THE ROUTE OF
ICE
&
SALT

JOSÉ LUIS ZÁRATE

TRANSLATED BY DAVID BOWLES

Published by Innsmouth Free Press
Vancouver, BC Canada
innsmouthfreepress.com

ISBN paperback: 978-1-927990-29-2
ISBN e-book: 978-1-927990-30-8

Cover illustration: Gustave Doré
Cover design: Innsmouth Free Press
Interior design and e-book design: Ampersand Book Interiors

INTRODUCTION

FIRST PUBLISHED IN 1998 by Grupo Editorial Vid
in Mexico, *The Route of Ice and Salt* (*La Ruta del Hielo
y la Sal*) was an oddity for several reasons. Grupo Editorial Vid was known for publishing comic books but
was attempting to launch a line of science fiction and
fantasy novels by Mexican authors. Most science fiction
and fantasy in Mexico at that time – and still today –
was imported and translated from the English language.

José Luis Zárate was an emerging writer in a small,
tight-knit circle of science fiction and fantasy authors
scattered across Mexico. His choice of subject matter was
unorthodox in two ways: One, he was writing an episto-
lary take on *Dracula*. Two, it was a queer novella.

El Vampiro de la Colonia Roma, which, despite the title,
is not about a vampire, had been published in 1979 and

caused a sensation by focusing on the life of a young, gay man navigating the city. In 1998, gay rights had advanced and the Zona Rosa was a clubbing area for queer Mexico City youth, but finding queer characters in books, movies and TV was still a difficult task. *The Route of Ice and Salt* was a horror book but one with literary aspirations; a novel about queer desire, it was being released by an editorial imprint that had never published anything like it.

Grupo Editorial Vid's goal of entering the book market ultimately failed. Science fiction and fantasy did not take much of a foothold in Mexican bookstores, where the only horror books available continued to be bestsellers by Stephen King and 19th century classics like, yes, *Dracula*.

Zárate went on to write more stories of the fantastic and also taught literature in his native Puebla. *The Route of Ice and Salt* became something of a cult item for Spanish science fiction and fantasy readers. It was eventually translated into French, and is now being presented in English for the very first time.

Along with this translation by David Bowles, there is a new prologue by the author and an afterword by Poppy Z. Brite. I hope this provides readers with a full picture of a book that has occupied an important place in Latin American literature of the fantastic yet which has nonetheless remained largely unknown to English speakers.

— Silvia Moreno-Garcia, 2020
Canada

PROLOGUE

THE RAIN WAKES me up. Not because it is strong or dense - it wakes me because, without knowing, I've been waiting for it.

It's a late rain. The cold has begun and winter is in the air.

I look at the clock at my side - 3 a.m. - but I twist it away because the glow of the LED doesn't go well with the primordial murmur of the water. I get up and stretch my hand towards my clothes, but don't complete the gesture.

I go to the patio; to the darkness.

There's no more noise than the sound of water, and in that moment it is just my skin and the rain. I close my eyes, lift my face and wait.

The intimate warmth of the bed disappears in an instant.

I feel over me a slow caress. The water travels as if it wants to discover every centimeter of me.

The caress of a dead hand. A hungry embrace, fierce in its impatience to encompass me.

My body reacts to the contact, shivering, but at the same time, absolutely conscious of each part of me.

Here I am, practically nude.

Here I am, in the storm.

I shiver and I do not know if it is from pleasure or fright.

Perfect, I tell myself, returning to my bed.

I have a thread for my novel.

The story I wish to tell is a ghost walking the hallways of my mind. I can't see it completely, but I know it's there and I search for a way to make it discernible, concrete.

I read, without yet knowing why, stories of cursed voyages, the sad destiny of Arthur Gordon Pym, and the last lines of *Moby Dick*, where fury ends in disaster.

I take out the old VHS tapes and sit down late at night to watch the symphony in black, white and gray that is *Nosferatu*. One scene in particular: While the captain ties himself quickly to the rudder, Count Orlock approaches, full of power, hands like claws, the appearance of a human rat, surrounded by an air of disease and plague.

On the wall of my office, I stick a map torn from an atlas. I have marked with ink the trip that leads from Varna to Whitby; I look at it obsessively.

A trip from yesterday to today.

A past rabidly alive.

I mark all the countries to which the unfortunate schooner sails and I wonder what hungry yesterdays inhabit each one of them. What creatures, beings and spectres have been imagined, which come from death to feed on the living?

I sleep well, thinking of nightmares.

I sail towards them, in the midst of the storm and the furious waters.

A boat. A schooner. The *Demeter*.

I picture that name in the wood, gnawed by the salt.

And aren't the sailors surrounded by it? What flavor do the sailors possess for the vampire? Salt, of course, of the sea, of the sweat and the skin, of the blood and every secret liquid, intimate, sheltered by the body.

And if someone else desires it?

What if someone faces the vampire in order to save, to taste, to love that salt?

And who else is most appropriate to fight for those men than the captain of the boat?

A homosexual captain.

I think about what it means to be one on a Russian schooner of the 19th century. In those days, it was easy to be lynched for the mere crime of *being*. While I walk through the streets of my city, I think and observe, and discover that 1996 is not that far from the 19th century.

Many stories of the sea are stories of increasing growth, of the young person who acquires, through penuries and adventures, the security that allows them to leave their adolescence behind.

But what I am writing is a voyage of the damned.

And if I make it a story about decreasing? What if I snatch away the security and tranquility of the captain?

How cruel is the phantom of my interior.

Why write horror stories, stories of fear and darkness?

Most of the time, when people have asked me this question, it's a complaint. There are more important things than monsters, they tell me implicitly. I wish I could believe them ....

I was born in 1966 and I ignored everything. At bedtime, nobody tells children dark stories of power and repression, nor that a murderous tyranny governs us. I was busy learning how to walk, busy with my first words, happily protected and unaware.

The judicial police had the power of impunity. They could do whatever they wanted without repercussion.

They could claim that each one of their victims was guilty of political crimes.

This combination of hitmen and cops were called "madrinas" and they circulated freely through the streets. That you were innocent of everything couldn't protect you.

Children know even if they don't know. They may not understand the context, but the evidence is there.

I could not understand the conversation of the adults, but I understood the tone of their voices; the pauses filled with meaning and the heavy silence they forced upon themselves.

I remember, yes, the nocturnal glow of a television (black-and-white, with only two channels), and a movie where a silhouette of something shows against the window that protects the people from the night. A second before the glass breaks and the inconceivable darkness devours them, there is a pause, a silence.

The space of horror just before the bestial maw and blood.

The silence heard again and again from the adults.

Why do you write horror and not reality?

Why write a vampire story?

Back then, it seems, everyone loved vampires. Not old Lugosi, but David Bowie, modern and Gothic. The publicity for the film *The Lost Boys* proclaimed, "Sleep all day. Party all night. Never grow old. Never die. It's fun to be a vampire." The game of *Masquerade* showed us the sons of Cain, sophisticated and filled with a security born of knowing themselves masters of the night. The last rebels, the urban pirates, whose fury, appetite and desire responded only to their will.

I couldn't love them. I was upset by so much power, so much carefree impunity ....

Oh, come on, they said. *Imagine yourself being a predator, carnivorous, the lion amongst the sheep.*

But I looked at my fluffy wool and told myself it was dangerous to love assassins.

And despite this, I was fascinated by that world. I don't know why.

I read about vampires, of the style found in the documents gathered in 1746 by Agustin Calmet, and found a fragment that fascinated me: the way of burying the impure.

You filled their mouths with rocks. They were decapitated. They were buried under crossroads so they remained lost forever and, as an added precaution, they were pierced with a stake. Not the cinematographical one, absurdly portable. The traditional stake was a clumsy lance, heavy and huge, which basically nailed the corpse to the ground, like a butterfly that should never fly again.

What kind of monsters deserved such treatment, such rage and contempt?

Vampires, yes, but also the bastard sons, the unbaptized ones, the inhabitants of other regions, the sodomites and those careless souls who allowed a black cat to jump over their dead bodies.

In short: anyone.

Anyone could be considered a monster. And monsters were assassinated with impunity.

Didn't you know? Didn't we all know? The grownups who hushed themselves to protect the children; the children who, without knowing how, discovered they were not safe from the darkness and death?

Perhaps that's what fascinated me about the topic. But not from the perspective of the assassin.

How would his shadow be perceived? What do the gazelles think of tigers? What sensations exist when one falls into a winter that one knows will never leave?

What does it feel like to walk down streets that can devour you any second, where impunity and prejudice can decide to finish you off without any cares?

What does it feel like when you sail towards a shipwreck?

– José Luis Zárate, 2020
Mexico

I AM WITNESS OF THAT BLOOD.

Efraín Huerta

DEMETER

FROM VARNA TO WHITBY

one

BEFORE
THE STORM

FROM 5 TO 16 JULY
1897

AT NIGHT: THE smell, the weight, the feel of salt.

Much more present than the water on the other side of the wood.

Who could have fathomed?

Nights spent, not in dreaming of sirens of uncertain sex, but in the eternal, tireless caress of the grains that lurk within the liquid.

When the midday sun dries the sails, dampened by breeze or storm, they crust over with that omnipresent granular white that seeps in with the salty mist of the night sea, finding its way into our hair, between our fingers.

No place is safe. It burrows into every crevice of the ship, into the metal bunks, into our provisions, into the treasures that we attempt to keep from rust. Its presence is a mocking smile.

And when the men strip away their clothing, they find it between their thighs, hidden where groin and testicles meet.

The sailors are Lot's wife.

Creatures of salt.

When I go to the forecastle, redolent with the absurd heat of bodies that rest in the midst of the swelter, I can almost see it accumulating on their indolent skin.

Who has tasted it? Who has savored ocean and flesh in that hidden place?

Not I.

I cannot.

I am the Captain.

Impossible that I order one of my men to come to my cabin and ask him to undress, much less insist he stand still and permit me to clean him with my tongue, lightly biting his flesh, trembling with craving for his skin.

And if there is no flavor?

That would mean that some other has saved him from the salt.

Then I should have to demand an accounting, impose discipline, require they reserve for me alone their salt, their warm sex.

But I cannot demand an accounting.

Not when the days are so long and we drift beneath the sun upon the windless water, measuring the hours by the slow drip of sweat.

In the distance, one can see the horizon move, a useless mirage: water in the midst of water, boiling.

At such moments, it is not difficult to imagine that we burn there.

How to deny them aught if these waters deny us all?

Is it not better to know that an immemorial hunger was satisfied, that one offered himself—entirely of his own volition—to an appetite that creates us as it devours us?

Their bodies are their own.

Not mine or of some possible lover.

Theirs that sweat and the sweat of any man to whom they grant it.

The salt of life ....

It is in those moments that I yearn for the icy routes. The Gulf of Botnia. The Baltic Sea. The North Sea.

Such strictures. The crew's rooms sealed. Men hidden in blankets and coats. Under siege, attempting to prevent the entry of the eternal, indifferent cold. We can slide over it or die upon it. It cares not.

Captains trapped in sudden ice, harkening to those deadly sounds—boats torn open by icy needles, metal giving way, crumpling under the weight of a million transparent blades—will not believe that the cold is not an enemy.

I have seen ice form on the horizon, huge landless isles drifting away from our route. The cycles of winter and snow have naught to do with the ships that cross their path.

The Northern Lights flare up and burn, though no man perceive them.

Ice is for other beings, its rhythms and reasons beyond our ken, its starkness for alien eyes.

The indifference of God, murmured by the world.

The cold suffices unto itself; the heat demands that we partake.

We can take refuge from the frost. It does not belong to us. We can cover ourselves with furs and approach the fire.

But what to do when the heat comes from within?

In the dead of night, our blood is like a sweat inside the body, warm sea nestled within our flesh, skin feverish and throbbing.

How to seek shelter from that which runs through our very veins?

Whoever dies frozen drifts away from his body, leaving in the midst of a merciful dream.

Whoever dies by fire remains trapped within that roiling flesh until the final moment, screaming until death comes like a balm.

Such notions occupy a man's thoughts beneath the motionless sun, when the shadows of the schooner are but warm shade. Steam rises from the waters. Sweltering air pursues us.

How delightful to walk naked in such heat.

But flesh fragments under the sun. First, cracks appear, then sores scoured by salt.

So, I must forbid it, order them to wear acidic clothes, astringent shirts, pants stiff with salt.

I ask them to seal themselves up with sultriness under those fabrics.

Not even below decks can I enjoy the sight of their bodies. If I stare too hard at them, they take my frank look as another order. They stand, saluting to their own chagrin before getting dressed to mine.

Their sweat (could it be otherwise?) makes me imagine firm muscles, taut veins.

Other captains ask why I choose men from certain lands, why sailors with exotic accents work with me.

I cannot answer with the truth, that it matters not to me whence they come, nor their race, nor the words that dwell in their tongues.

I look for smooth bodies, muscles along which sweat can freely run, liquid flowing, sliding.

Therefore, am I quite strict about their clothing.

For I know that beneath, there is almost no hair, naught to hinder wet caresses, fingers sketching desire.

Or eyes that also seem to touch the path of salt.

And so, I abandoned the glacial route, the seas of ice, the dark blue.

An ill decision.

But this I knew from the beginning.

The sun dries men, overwhelming them with its weight. It makes them aware of themselves, aware that they swim in some sweltering miasma.

Their flesh barely contained. Always present, whispering its appetites.

But a prison nonetheless.

Therefore, in the few icy ports that our route touches, we leave but a meager guard on the *Demeter*, seeking stone houses where we can breathe the cold.

Our territory: boundary between flesh and world. Cold without, we men within our skin.

And even there, despite our memories of the broiling sun, we long for fire.

We seek, then, the heat of other flesh. The salt on other skin.

My crew invites me to partake of wine and beer at their side. Sometimes, they sacrifice part of their wages to buy me such women as they find comely.

I choose the youngest ones, small-bosomed, resembling more children than females. The whiter the better.

But such specimens are dear and I dare not buy them for myself.

For hours, I close my eyes and imagine that other lips produce those caresses. I ask them not to speak, to stop being themselves, so that my fantasy may more readily transmute their flesh and I can achieve a weak, trembling orgasm that seems to escape from me, spilling out like sand.

The harlots prowling for crews are not unaware that—during the still hours upon the water, when all that exists is the certain solitude of darkest night and the slow breathing of the other sailors—one will seek, sooner or later, the taste of salt between the thighs.

And so, those women also sell their sons.

Devastated boys, like their mothers, beautiful only to newly landed men, their vision scorched by the sun, clouded by drink.

Sailors purchase such ephebes. Why should they not? It is no secret.

On the islands, the boys are sold more cheaply. It is not uncommon to find them in the ports along our route.

Is Greece not renowned for the practice?

But I do not buy them. I remain with my men, pretending to regard women, sharing anecdotes that matter little to anyone.

I cannot buy them.

Not when I accompany my crew.

I am the Captain. I hold in my hands the lives of my men.

My men.

Along the route of salt, murder and intrigue are simpler. Muscles burn and seek to give that burning some meaning. To move, to smash against something; to act.

Against what? Against what, in the midst of such stillness?

There can be no favoritism upon my schooner.

That is why I shall not choose any man. I shall never keep watch with those whom I desire. I refuse to let them walk naked.

I dare not.

Thence the difficulty of gathering my crews: hairless men from icy countries.

I prefer that the heat make them drowsy, that it be a heavy blanket over their heads. I do not want men accustomed to heat, whose brown skin can bear the full brunt of the noonday sun.

I do not wish them to laugh at my command to clothe themselves.

I should be wholly unable to get away from such men. I should never stop looking for the hidden taste within their bodies.

The salt of their seed.

Crews come and go. On each journey a new man, another who leaves.

They do well. I am not a good captain. Many things distract me.

They are uncomfortable with me. On a schooner, there is not room enough to dissemble their exasperation.

In Varna, I thought I should lose all my crew. After serving for a long time among the Southern Sporades in the Aegean Sea, supplying the Dodecanese Islands, they must be weary of the heat, of me, of the old *Demeter*, docked so many useless days in the port of Rhodes.

The Black Sea must have reminded them that they were men of cold climes; connoisseurs more of ports like Odessa, Sevastopol, Sochi, Batumi than of islands with strange names: Schinoussa, Nisyros, Laconia, Kalymnos.

I know (how not to know?) that they ache for white-skinned women who speak their tongues, that they are plagued by memories of frigid lands, of ice creaking in storm winds.

What could the women of the Greek islands know of the howling Baba Yaga, her ramshackle home creeping through snowy forests on looming rooster legs? Naught. Swarthy women will smile at such an image, unable to protect sailors from the fear that their mothers' whispers instilled in them during endless winter hours.

They should have left to seek those white bodies, those shared memories of ice. But they have remained, nigh-on to a man, at my side.

We have arrived in Bulgaria. They have gone ashore without asking for extra coin to sustain them while they find another ship.

They spend their hours in dark taverns, while the owners of the *Demeter* prepare contracts, organize another trip, trace another route for us.

When it is time to sail, the men will return to the schooner as if it were their home, the only familiar thing in the heart of such foreign lands.

They have not remained for me, for love of this old ship.

It is simply difficult to find other jobs. All are as bad as the previous one.

I should have preferred that they leave.

With every sailor who travels with me for the first time, there is a chance.

New blood is always necessary.

2

AT DUSK, A group of Tziganes arrived at the port.

Gypsies of coarse clothes and slow movements, hands full of cracks, eyes burned by the white glare of the snow.

Above the din of their mounts, they exchanged insults in a language that sounded harsh even amidst the cries and blasphemy of the men of the port.

They were not nomads. Their horses had but weapons tied to their saddles: sabers, knives, heavy muskets. There were no blankets, no tools for preparing hunted game.

They must return somewhere, after they deliver the cargo of the heavy carts they pull.

The port both disgusts and attracts them. They look upon the boats that sway in the foul waters much the way I look upon my crew.

These represent passage to some unfamiliar place, unknown in its possibilities, and therefore both frightening and full of promise.

They leave their horses nearby (without setting a watch, for who would dare take something from *them*? Who would challenge their steel?) and stare at the black sea from the pier.

In their eyes, distrust of the anchored wood of this place.

They are people of earth. They challenge it astride their mounts; they trace their paths like the skin of their lovers, skin as rough and dark as their own.

A traveling race, they love distances as I do the path of salt.

Yet, these few have remained for reasons I do not understand.

They treat the cargo with a care at odds with their nature, handling the boxes as if the wood might appreciate the delicacy they demand of themselves.

It is nearly a caress, with the fearful gesture of the blind near the fire.

How close to approach without danger; how close before pleasure becomes a fierce attack of heat?

A man oversees those who work. He does not protect them; each one, even amidst the grueling work of stowage, keeps a long saber at his side, always prepared for violence.

The man's duty instead is to glare at strangers, conveying a message to any who observe: *Do not dare call us servants.*

The way they seize the hilts of their swords implies that these are not mere blades in their hands, but extensions of their fury. They can split the air with them the way sailors clench their fists or hurl insults: without effort, as naturally and easily as breathing.

They have killed.

They have died killing.

One look at them suffices to reveal it.

They unload heavy boxes onto my ship, cursing in an ancient language known only to them, alien and dense as a threat.

And despite it all, they *are* servants.

Wild servants of some noble boyar.

Noble ....

A lord as wild as they. More so, as he has made them his vassals.

What might he have offered such men, who rip from the earth what they need? This proud race that fears not to die?

Something more than death.

Mayhap a different death. Perchance he has seduced them by offering something wilder than their own lives.

Upon the Wallachian Plain, are there still warrior lords who burn castles, advancing with their hordes through the dark snow?

What do these men have to do with the *Demeter*? With the orders neatly signed by the owners of my ship? A noble boyar who owns an army of Tziganes, with S. F. Billington, a solicitor from England?

It is not my duty to discover the truth.

Only to transport the crates piling up in the hold.

I watch them work, saying naught. I do not grasp why they must unload the merchandise solely at night. We should look like smugglers were it not for the fact that the people of Varna examine each box and scrutinize the paperwork thoroughly, looking for irregularities. It makes no matter that there is naught out of place; they will find some trivial error and ask for the small bribe they consider their just dessert after rifling through the merchandise, shuddering against the cold, while the fog approaches at low tide as if it has secreted something away in its wispy skirts.

I wonder how they intend to make the Tziganes pay for some trifling detail.

Will they dare?

But all that happens on land.

Meanwhile, I wait on my ship, silent.

Mayhap they assume that my silence has some meaning.

Mayhap it does.

They look at me, they pass me by, but they never try to threaten me with their presence.

They know that I am the noble boyar of my ship; the absolute lord of the demesne delimited by the schooner's wooden hull.

They respect me for that.

Lord of a movable demesne.

They are within my borders. They were ordered to enter. They know not where my warriors be, whether they wait in some hiding place only I can descry. This land is mine and mine its secrets.

I could order their deaths and they would not argue the justice of the act.

Their world does not work thus.

They are gypsy slaves, though no one says they are. They have offered their fates, the fates of their families, to some puissant Lord.

I watch them work and wonder what commands they would obey or cease to obey.

How completely does their Master own their lives?

If he asked them, would they kill their own children ... would they fall on their swords, would they open their veins for him?

Would they stay still if he arrived with a gun, with his member ready to penetrate them?

They see me watching them.

Do they believe I can do the same with my sailors? That I tread my lands with no more rein than my desires, free to play with life and death?

How enslaved are they?

They must deliver the cargo .... at what cost?

Inexplicably, unable to avoid the impulse, I approach them.

I have to touch them.

If I am a boyar, they should be instruments. I watch them as if they were things.

They are not. They are living flesh, movement, warm sweat ....

But their decisions are no longer theirs. Puppets of firm faces, of naked necks that tense while they work, highlighting their skin, which invites me ....

I approach one of them and touch his neck because he wears no expression; rough, wiry, tense, all he communicates is strength.

It is akin to touching greasy wood, the damp heat of work under my palm.

I stroke him, running my fingers gently over that skin.

Now is precisely when the Tzigane should pull my hand away, unsheathing his steel and slicing my neck.

This should be the moment I begin to fear.

And I do. I fear the desperation with which my hand touches that skin, the hunger of my fingers, the erection this contact awakens.

The skin under my palm also shudders, tenses and pulls away as if I were transmitting cold, as if a living statue had reached out to touch the man.

Pleasure and fear sometimes resemble each other greatly.

He raises his eyes to meet mine.

I read them without understanding.

Continue, stop.

He has not turned away, he has done nothing, nor does he stir at all as I slowly lean toward him.

A muscle jumps in his face, only one, which then sinks into his flesh as if trying to flee from me.

Boyar.

Voivode.

Master ....

I bring my lips to his neck and touch his salt.

My tongue a blade, a short finger that digs into his skin. Rough, earthy, bitter. And at that moment, mine. I surround it with my mouth, savoring that flesh intimately before slowly pulling away, letting my lips caress it, spiraling upon those muscles in smaller and smaller circles, until I withdraw, leaving a small trace of saliva.

I am still there. The saliva on the neck of that man insists that I am still there.

Yet, only my hand remains upon him, gripping his neck.

I notice how the Tzigane leans against the box that moments before he had been pushing into place. His legs tremble.

Not from humiliation. These men know what to do with one who humiliates them. Their steel has learned to act.

The others regard us and, in their eyes, there is no message, nothing. As if they were watching the snow fall upon them, an avalanche that they cannot halt and that, in some way, is part of their lives: the immovable fact.

Unjudgeable.

What has happened between that Tzigane and me has joined us in their eyes. We partake of a rite from which they are excluded.

A rite beyond my ken, though I have commenced it.

I cannot understand. I have on my tongue the taste of an unknown skin, bitter and sweet at the same time. I slowly pet the man's neck as if stroking the muzzle of a horse. Then I release him, stepping back.

The Tzigane mutters something and continues his work. All of them do. No one draws away from him when he approaches.

I have not stained him with my caress. The man has come away clean from my lips.

Can your Master's command free you men from guilt?

Or is what happened here infinitely less than what ye expected?

Would ye show the same indifference had I cut his throat?

Once, only once, they turn to regard me.

The noble boyar of the Demeter.

I should like to believe it ....

3

When the wind bites the sails and the wood slips steady through the water, free of the waves that pound the harbor—at that moment, I know we have begun our journey.

I note *July 6* in the log, but that date says nothing. *Twelve o'clock on the hour, with a cold east wind.* Data only.

Not a gray sky, not the steel-colored sea surrounded by a persistent fog that should not remain at noon. Not the shouts of my sailors while they work the sails.

Facts scrawled in ink, without real meaning.

The crew consists of five men, two deck officers, the cook, and me.

Men from Russia, Vojvodina, Slovenia, Dalmatia, and Romania.

We leave the port of Varna, entering the Black Sea, on a route that will lead us from the East to cross the Aegean Sea, the Mediterranean, hugging the European coast before at last coming to port in England.

The route of ice and salt.

The gypsies, on their mounts, watched our movements and the actions of those who remained on land. Their dark hands gripped drawn weapons, at the ready, as if expecting that someone might attempt to stop us, prepared to repel any attack, willing to offer their blood in exchange for our safe departure.

An honor guard: excessive protection for a few boxes of clay and dirt.

What orders did they receive, precisely?

My second officer, Muresh, heard that the gypsies had arrived in Varna at noon yesterday, that they had stood at the entrance of the port, under the sun, for hours, indifferent to the slow passing of men and animals that brushed by them without ceasing.

Those men of the steppes, of the frozen horizon, hate the touch of strangers and - nevertheless - they remained there, waiting until nightfall to deliver their cargo.

Why?

The man who commanded them looked me in the eye a second before we set sail.

That I had touched one of his men was an affront. That he could not take revenge was a greater stigma still.

I had declared them slaves, servants.

And my blood had escaped them.

They looked upon me with infinite hatred, in which I could descry the free land they had lost, the lives without shadows they offered in exchange for something much more valuable than their pride, the one quality that has always sustained them in so many lands that were never theirs.

The chief Tzigane uncovered his neck with a slight gesture of defiance.

Mayhap he wished to convey that had his master not told them that those boxes must set sail, I should be dead for touching one of his men.

Or mayhap the message was another. Perchance he signaled that the taste of their skins was the right of another.

Not their own. Never their own.

Yet, until their master claimed that right, their flesh still belonged to them, completely.

As soon as we left the port, once the moorings were coiled and stowed, when it became clear that his mission was over, the Tzigane shouted something, a phrase.

His voice reached me weak, void of nuance. Mayhap a message, an explanation, an insult, a terrible truth.

"*Denn die Todten reiten schnell!*"

Then he spurred the horses, and he and his men galloped away.

The ominous words echoed in my heart:

"For the dead travel fast."

4

THE WORLD HAS shrunk by becoming immense.

We have left the coast behind, and the horizon is but a blend of sea and sky.

Gray, endless sky. Dark, bottomless sea.

One can get lost in them. This we all know. We remember, without knowing why, the names of ships and crews that reached their final port in the depths of that watery abyss.

We are alone with our schooner.

We shield ourselves from infinity with the wood of the ship, with the sails and thrumming lines that grip the wind. With our muscles under the sun, with the thundering orders of the First Mate.

We check the cargo, tightening the tense ropes as if we could secure our position, reinforce the certainty that we shall remain here, though the scale and indifference of our surroundings threaten to unmoor our minds.

Then do we remember.

Always late.

The world is naught but these men, the deck, the cellar, the gunwales, the hatches, the cabins.

We have reduced the universe to what lies between stem and stern.

To fall into the water is to leave the world.

That the world might leave us is equally unimaginable.

It must remain with us. The schooner floats firmly upon our faith that she will always be here. The notion that she might shipwreck, that the waters might penetrate her interior, is as inconceivable as that the sky might crack open, letting black nothingness swirl into the world.

Yet, it has happened.

Boats becoming coral; men feeding fish never lit by the sun.

Such truths I do not mention, do not scrawl with fresh ink.

The Captain's log is no company, either.

Those entries I compose for the ship owners and the men who will inherit this ship when I retire.

The voice that I offer to the memory of the trip is different. To read it is to meet another man who is yet me. A man who speaks only of facts, of details devoid of nuance.

At dusk, I go on deck and I hear the men who stayed on guard speak. They do not pronounce words because they have something meaningful to share, but because silence sits heavy on our hearts when we know it looms larger than we.

The *Demeter* speaks. We know her language, her creaking chatter, her canvas whispers, her dry words of wood. Her voice is for us; we summon it when we push her with the wind, when we mark a route for her.

She tells me that all is well, that we leave behind knots and miles and kilometers, that she advances toward the coasts of Turkey as if something we wanted awaits us there.

5

The first night.

The day's labor complete. A man at the helm, surrounded by lighted lamps that illuminate the immense darkness on which we sail. Dinner inside us, still warm, just stocked, the water untainted and the bread fresh.

Us, floating in our beds, upon that fatigue into which we can sink, clinging to the blankets so as not to drown in dreams.

There is no sound save the waves without, the snapping of the sails, the slow groaning of wood struggling to remain joined. Closer still, someone's breathing, the only person in this cabin.

Me.

The cold enters uninterrupted through the open door. The slow movement of the schooner makes the door swing open and shut with nigh-on no sound. An eye that blinks. What does it see? A man who cannot sleep, a dark hallway.

In another place, a different eye looks upon the crew, submerged in the heat of their fatigue, the scent of their bodies a warm mist which no one disturbs.

I put my hand over my mouth, slowly open my lips, moistening my palm.

I feel my nascent beard, my rough skin, my saliva.

I slowly squeeze my cheekbones.

Were my hand but free; were there no will directing it ….

I am two skins: the one that brushes closer and the one that awaits.

But both are none, because I know who controls them.

At times, as if in dreams, I imagine that I raise my hands to find I can sink them into the night. If I make two fists, I can all but feel it slide between my fingers like a slow oil.

There is no way to catch it, to rip off a piece. Nor do I want to. Only to feel it.

I sink myself into that night; a lifeless breath against my visage, a leviathan mouth that absorbs me.

I open my lips, wishing to drown in these sensations.

Darkness is a whole, indivisible, without members. A body unto itself, uninterrupted.

I yank the sheets aside, impatiently tearing the clothes from my body and with them, the heat I have nestled close.

I arch my back on my cot. I can feel the stitch of the fabric beneath me, but it matters not. Only my chest as it surges into the night, the slow liquid sliding, an icy breath running along my muscles, lingering on my nipples.

I sink my sex into that dark flesh that neither draws back nor opens, that throbs at my entrance without ever moistening me.

I sink into that nothing, while my own sex, tumescent, spreads the skin that covers it, as if by its own will, as if an invisible hand gently pulled back the dark prepuce.

The icy sensation is no caress; it is something that happens to another, that has naught to do with me. Nor does that throbbing member. Sterile in nothingness, abandoned in silence.

Nothing caresses it. Nothing touches it, yet still it hardens. Yet still I feel it taut against its skin, as if it might burst, might tear itself open with desperation.

I cannot long maintain that position. I drop back into bed, into reality.

I touch myself, questing for a liquid that does not exist, the cold oil of the darkness, but there is only my skin, which is still no skin, only that which covers my body. A living sheet.

I touch my sex.

So sensitive that I shudder, fingers at the base, along the wrinkled flesh, on the moistened foreskin that waits in vain. I do not caress myself.

To what end?

I have drawn away from any sensation; all that passes is time, minute by minute.

Every first night is the same.

Not tonight.

I dare not close my eyes. I shall not let the dream come to me.

And yet, my eyelids close by themselves, as if an invisible hand forces them to do so.

To sleep is to abandon oneself to darkness.

Around me the workaday noises, the sea beyond the wood, my own stirring self. A ship in the void.

*I feel that something, **someone**, enters the cabin. Is that not why I never close my door?*

I await.

I, transformed into a servant of another skin that may leave me free of blame.

I shall do nothing, I shall not even move until those other lips commence to touch me.

But they never do.

I should like to open my eyes, see who stands in the doorway.

There must be wind out there. I feel a cold current that must envelop my visitor.

I can almost feel his icy silhouette, waiting.

Yet, it could all be a dream: those sliding steps, the whisper of fine fabrics around me, the slight-but-unmistakable smell of earth, but also of fresh linen that has not been dampened a million times.

The lips touching my lips, slippery with that dense moisture that only semen or blood possesses.

It must be a dream, for those lips are dead.

*The residents of the island of Thera claim that thus arrive the **vrykolakas**, with slow and delicate steps, furtive, taking care that the claws of their feet never scrape the wood, never wake those whom they stalk with incandescent eyes.*

When they reach their victim's side, they unfold an incredibly long arm, reaching for the ceiling, finding some sturdy place that can support their weight, and then they cling to this perch, hanging over the sleeper with an infinite delicacy, not wishing to wake him, to have his eyes open to look upon their black faces.

As a caress settles lightly on one's chest, so they crouch in the air, sinking their nails into the fresh flesh of their victim.

There they remain, stealing his breath, lowering their weight gradually-yet-inexorably, till at last they let go of their perch and settle firmly in the sleeper's dreams.

It is a time for stealing the soul. When we abandon our bodies to their own devices, leaving behind the specific appetites of the flesh.

*The sleep produced by the **vrykolakas** is heavy and dense, oppressive.*

Whoever becomes their victim dreams of dark waters that separate him from the world, of heavy shadows that know too much, of sins for which we cannot forgive ourselves, which stare at us with black faces and incandescent eyes.

The sailor of Thera said it:

*"The **vrykolakas** are suicides, apostates, the excommunicated, those who practiced dark magic, those whose corpses a cat crossed over, those who died violently, those murdered and never avenged, those conceived during the Major Holidays, those who have eaten meat of sheep killed by wolves, those who lived immorally."*

They are all of us.

I, as well.

In the dark waters of sleep, it was I who approached, as I did in reality, a man asleep in my bed.

I had not invited him to sleep there. He lay not upon that warm bed for me, to give me caresses or pleasure.

He simply was there and I could do nothing about it. I was little more than a child.

My sex stood out from my clothes as I approached that stranger.

They introduced him to us, affirming he was our cousin Mikhail.

But that was a lie.

Mikhail was there for reasons we did not understand. His presence was the payment of some secret debt. Someone we hid without knowing why.

Who explains things to children?

They can but accept them. And my body accepted him, agreed to shelter the stranger in the privacy of my sheets.

With a price ....

The dream feeds on my memories of the night when I approached that stranger, the figure hidden under the sheets, my teeth chattering with desire tempered by fear, armed with the curious power of which I was now owner.

He needed shelter.

The feeling that something fundamental would change the moment I pressed my naked body against the intruder.

I approached ....

Not afraid to wake him, but slowly, sinuously.

Yearning for him to hear me, to realize I was there, to assess the value of his security.

A figure under sheets, a young man hidden within them, with rough clothes that I must needs strip away, buttons and laces between him and my hands; old wool, the skin of dead animals hiding his living skin. Myself hidden in clothes. Only my sex was as free as I wanted our bodies to be.

*But in the **vrykolakas**' heavy dream, something had changed: the images were different.*

I lived a new reality.

I approached that bed knowing that the form hidden under the sheets was not that of a man.

There was something amiss, a detail that was not natural.

It *was awake, restless, moving as if the sheet were the thin membrane of a cracked egg, a web the creature was spinning, an integral part of the thing that awaited me there, hungry.*

And though I knew this, I ignored it.

I addressed it as if it were still Mikhail and I stood there, erect, approaching.

I touched the sheet.

More than warm: feverish, throbbing. I jerked it away because I could not help myself.

A rat.

There was a rat trapped under the bedclothes, frantic to escape. A ship rat, fat and dangerous, without fear of sailors or clubs, as huge as they say the largest grow, virtually without legs because they are not necessary in the midst of so much food, with massive teeth and mad eyes.

A rat willing to jump upon anything.

And I, desire tightening my chest, ignoring the danger, bringing my sex closer to the creature.

Jerking the sheets away ....

A sudden movement toward my cock and before I awaken to find myself screaming, the immediate pain, terrible.

I glance at my crotch, expecting to find blood, ribbons of bloody meat.

Just a white spot, the dusty scent of my semen.

7

GOING OUT IN the sun is a necessity, though the dawn mists retain some trace of darkness and sea within them.

Going out to a fading fray.

I behold the waters and they are no different from the fog that surrounds me. Dawn in the distance, as though it had naught to do with us.

The waters begin to lose consistency; they are no longer liquid shadows under the *Demeter*, but depths, an abyss over which we sail.

Joachim is at the helm, vigilant, and Acketz examines something in the gunwales. Too active, despite the changing of the watch.

They should be nearly still, yearning for the warmth of their blankets, a cup of rum inside them, hungry for some lively bare skin to free them from the cold in their bones, from the moisture that has seeped under their clothes.

But they work under the weight of the First Mate's watchful eye.

They fear him. They know that Vlahutza firmly believes that pain is the best argument.

They glance at him askance, hoping he is also tired, that the night hours have chipped away at him.

But the Romanian treads the bridge as though he will never tire.

He looks more a captain than I.

He is warmly swaddled, but his clothes have not bunched up upon his body; disciplined, they cover him, giving him a martial appearance. His shirt clings to his shoulders, his strong chest, his broad arms, his thick neck; pantaloons that embrace his legs, tucked inside his leather boots, hugging his narrow hips, molded lightly to the bulge of his sex.

He looks good.

He hides not in his coat. He carries it upon him, an instrument to defend himself from the weather, like unto the instruments of his warm blood, his strength, those hard muscles that ripple.

His clothes are not a heap of skins on some common body. I repeat, he is not me.

Upon seeing me, he gives a short gesture of greeting. It is not that he wishes to greet me, but that I am the Captain, and such is his duty.

He believes in the chain of command, that there is a logic to my assignments.

In taverns, captains are wont to declare: "*Aboard my ship, there is only God above me. But as long as God does not approach, I am the one in charge.*"

He believes in the insignia of the uniforms we seldom wear.

I am the Captain of the schooner and above me there is only God, but before the Captain is he.

He need only ascend two rungs to be God.

I contemplate his face. Strong and firm. The cold has ruddied his skin. Under his beard, one can descry the enduring freshness of his face. It is but the fourth day of sailing and the *Demeter* glides smoothly through the waters.

I like his face, his firm jaw, the muscle that twitches in his cheek when something bothers him.

He is stone, rock. I know.

I should like to penetrate that hardness, enter its warm interior, ejaculate inside it, seeking to dilute the sand that composes it.

I am not unaware that he might kill me if I try.

Aboard the ship that is his body, above him there is not even God.

I know not whether he enjoys the women he buys. I have seen him lead them away from the tavern with near indifference.

The chain of command, the insignias: He has the money they want; they have the sex he requires. He offers both copper coins and semen.

His caressing a woman in the presence of the other sailors is not meant to excite or please them: It is a way of telling us that the deal is made.

Grim kisses, tongue forcing lips open, no pleasure for either. Grim struggles to feel the merchandise.

"Captain," he says when I reach the bridge.

"Vlahutza."

He looks at me carefully, mayhap wondering whether I have awakened screaming from another nightmare, like the first night.

With a gesture, I say no, but I did scream. I know not whether in wakefulness or in sleep. My throat is dry and sore, but this proves nothing. Fear spreads salt in the lungs, dries out the mouth, makes saliva bitter.

I examine the deck as though making certain all is in order, that he has carried out accordingly all his nightly tasks.

I am all-but contemptuous. There is no sense in revealing that the same fear that infuses the sailors snarls in his Captain's heart.

8

I WALK THE schooner, stroking its wood, afraid that it will erode to dust between my fingers, like touching the fragile membrane of a dream, till it bursts and I awaken to discover myself alone in the water, the *Demeter* merely the beautiful fantasy of a drowning man.

There is naught but the harsh whisper of my fingers running along the grain, the hollows, the pockmarks in the flesh of my ship.

Are you well?

But one cannot inquire thus of inanimate things, of the corpses on which we travel the world.

One must instead examine each rope, touch the sails, harken unto the precise rhythm of the vessel. Certify that the dark sea does not penetrate the dead wood, that there is no other influx of water than our own anxiety.

I regard the sky above our heads, searching.

Something feels wrong, as though there is something amiss aboard our ship. Things are not as they should be.

Yet, they never are.

And in the sky, there is nothing. Not even *strigoi* wheeling down in search of live meat. The demonic birds of the night, Vlahutza once told me, mocking the very notion of such things. Mocking his father, who had smeared garlic on his flesh to ward them off, to keep that unimaginable bird-shaped darkness from taking him away. *They have no body*, his father told him. *They should not be able to grip anything. They are night, simply, holes in reality, and they want naught but a little blood. Those who survive their attack bear black wounds that, it is said, ooze only cold. They appear after sunset, in the ocean of darkness, a darkness that spreads with hunger ... which seeks human flesh, and the setting of the sun is but a flood of those birds.*

The night, a single *strigoi* devouring the world.

At times, I wonder whether a concrete fear is better, whether that swath of deadly night lowering upon us is preferable to the ineffable nothing gnawing at our nerves.

To the strange certainty that we have left a door open somewhere, an unwitting invitation to whatever awaits outside, stalking us.

I recall the successive snows of winter, creaking on the roofs, ever promising, whispering to the child I was then of how the wide sky was collapsing upon our house. The neighbor who lost a finger to the gelid cold, the knowledge that to become lost in the snow meant the surety of splintering, of shattering like a glass full of blood.

Before a blizzard, I should look upon the dark earth for what seemed the last time, before the punctillated pattern of white made it something else entirely. Such helplessness in seeing the warm, familiar, kindly autumn world swallowed bit by bit.

On the deck of the *Demeter*, looking out upon the sea and the non-existent *strigoi*, I felt everything disappear under a snowfall that no one else perceived. Without yet knowing why, I was certain that, somehow, Winter had embarked with us.

9

By the fifth day, the routines and behaviors we must perform daily are fully established. The dogged watches, crew assignments, navigational charts for the hours we must spend on board.

Tour the ship again, survey the ropes that secure the cargo, the sterile load in our hold. Fifty boxes of earth. In the permits, someone has scrawled "for scientific experiments" as sufficient justification. Our schooner was hired to carry solely these. There will be no port that interrupts the trip from Bulgaria to England.

The forecastle and sterncastle, occupied by crew and officers. The sailors have already hidden a bit of their rations there, oil has been spilled inadvertently on the deck, their clothes have surrendered to the ineluctable march of disorder.

On my table, the papers will multiply. The instruments for dead reckoning will hide among them. The heavy stench of smoke and liquor will permeate every nook along with the spicy aroma of the food that Arghezi prepares, stirred by the constant comings and goings to follow orders and ease the tedium.

Today, when darkness brings no sleep, stories will be told, false memories of non-existent women desperately offering themselves to the men of the *Demeter*.

The First Mate will be discussed for the first time, while someone peers at the bruises raised by Vlahutza's handspike. Rancor will ferment from this moment on.

At night, the furtive sounds will begin, self-caresses that seek to slake desire.

Routines I must miss.

My position keeps me from approaching them when they eat, from listening to their slow anecdotes in the dim light, from remaining within the forecastle with the constant flood of their scent.

I am the Captain, Lord of this house while at sea. And there is the First Mate to remind me and frown when I talk more with any of the men.

It is not my role to speak: I am master to them all, momentary slaves of port pay.

But they are not mine.

I also have a master: the owners of the *Demeter*. Their offices in Russia, where rest documents in which I swear to avoid problems, where my slaves could denounce me should I give in to my appetites.

I must carry out my own routines.

Serve the food to the officers in their cabins; be the daily host of my Second Mate.

Knowing that Vlahutza hates those moments, I do not oblige him to join us. Therefore, is he my First Officer: It is his wont to walk the bridge and govern the ship while I eat, for surely while there is a Master up there, my presence is not required.

Arghez. I shall take rations to him, or he will descend later to eat alone, with no more company than the ship rats and the waves just beyond the wood.

The cook disappears after serving the food. Muresh relaxes while pouring wine into a glass and I tell myself that it is strange to be alone with him.

I look him in the eye and almost manage to smile. I slice away the best cut of meat (warm blood, steaming seasoned crust, the tenderness of a little fat) and serve it as though it were a favor he cannot comprehend.

Many times, when I go back out to the bridge, Vlahutza glances pointedly at his watch.

So much time to finish so little food?

How to explain that time matters not when our mouths and guts are full of meat and wine?

We revel in the simple communion of the senses.

The delicate taste that blossoms when biting the meat, the dry aroma of the drink, the feel of one's tongue gliding through one's mouth, the satisfied sound of one's body feeding.

Gluttony is a capital sin, one I can understand each afternoon, every time I give a bit of my food to the Second Mate, an added pleasure to serve as host.

Intimacy, bodies finding satisfaction together, never touching but united in the common act.

Just Muresh and I. Sharing that simple daily meal. Intimate, nigh-on conjugal, as though such moments brought us closer in some fashion. Then I can almost pretend that I have spent the night with the man I feed, that we rest from our pleasure with the pleasure of breaking bread.

If, to feel that intimacy, it suffices that we be isolated from the rest of the crew, what then does it mean that we nine men of the *Demeter* have separated ourselves from the world?

What does being alone in the middle of the ocean make us?

IO

"THE COASTS OF Turkey, sir," says Muresh, when dawn shows us the horizon broken by a line of land.

I observe the entrance to the Bosphorus Strait with such attention that the Second Mate looks again for something new. But he finds only the *felucca* of Turkish customs maneuvering to reach our ship.

I order the First Mate to reduce speed.

I touch the bag hidden in my clothes, the coins arranged since the start of our voyage for the taxes we must pay for the greater glory of Sultan Abdul-Hamid II. And the obligatory bribe.

The old ceremony. Receive the officers. Hand over the documents they will review with suspicion, the brief review of the *Demeter*, the discovery of some detail that will make our old schooner a danger to other ships sailing to the Marmara Sea, the fact that they at last forgive us magnanimously this defect and allow us to continue, the farewell in which I give them additional coin. Never a bribe, only a recognition of their generosity.

A ceremony that will occupy us nearly the entire day.

The chief of the men who board us is Captain Melih and when he sees our flag, he mentions, quite matter-of-factly, that his father was killed by a Russian, during the war.

I mentally add a few more coins to the bribe.

He glances around as though he could glean our intentions from our mere appearance. I look at my crew; there is nary a suspicious thing about them.

Mayhap Abranoff's tired appearance as he, like his Captain, has not slept well these last few nights. Or the familiarity with which Petrofsky and Acketz stand close together. Or the serious mien of Vlahutza.

He asks me to accompany him below to survey the cargo.

He has a couple of his men go down first, then he follows, a lamp in one hand and a pistol in the other. It is not a firm, self-confident gesture, like that of Varna's Tziganes.

In the hold, there are only the boxes and a few dead gray rats on the floor. Naught else.

The Turk looks at me accusingly, as though I had put those small corpses there just to make him uncomfortable.

I must treat the rats as an unimportant curiosity; otherwise, the *baksheesh* will be unusually large. And we did not bring enough money to afford it.

I pick one up with indifference and examine it briefly.

"Old rats," I say, tossing it into a corner, not letting disgust cloud my face, for the animal seems a bag devoid of weight, drained, internal organs gnawed. A shell.

Alongside Captain Melih, I examine the boxes we are transporting.

Wood: sturdy and well-assembled.

Too much so.

Only at that moment do I realize the strange construction of the crates. Valuable wood, with a triple row of nails ensuring it will not come apart for any reason.

No simple packaging, shipping containers; I should almost classify them as furniture, built with precision, with a particular purpose in mind.

There is no defect, except a small crack running the length of some lids.

While the Turks count the boxes, I run my fingers along the tiny imperfection.

It is akin to caressing skin: firm, soft, rounded ... I consider it again. Too precise; an idealized drawing of a crack.

Without knowing why, I close my eyes, draw the crack upon my palm, letting the feel of it travel the lines of my hand. It is difficult, soft ... I trace it and the motion makes it easier to form an image of it ....

I carry that image between my fingers, transport it to another crack, a different crate with another imperfection. I touch the new lid, resting my hand upon it, closing my eyes.

The cracks are identical, as if sketched upon the wood itself, without any variation.

Not a defect. Put there deliberately.

Someone hid the precise purpose of that drawing by disguising it. But to what end? It is too small to serve as ventilation. As tiny as the path of the worms inside an apple. I imagine them wriggling their way out of the box, joining together under my palm to form a rat, its fur a million white worms squirming, blinking a million blind eyes.

A rat like the one waiting under my sheets, every night.

Something infinitely small grazes my hand, digging into the whorls of my fingertips, humid and agile like some infinitesimal tongue ....

With a shout, I jerk my hand away from the box. Melih looks up from a document and walks toward me.

He can confiscate the cargo, my ship, hold us in this place for as long as he deems necessary, lock us in the schooner with these boxes for months entire.

Not expecting the effort it requires, I shake my hand with a gesture of pain. Although I can still perceive something viscous on my fingertips, I bring it to my lips ....

A splinter.

As though unconscious of his stare, I dig with my teeth for a non-existent fragment stuck in my skin. After I feign its extraction, I sigh, bored, and look around.

Melih continues reading the permits, reviewing the stamps.

There is nothing unusual. Not *there*, at least.

At 4:00 pm, we receive the order to continue our course. I write in the log with a firm gesture: *All correct.*

I do not believe so.

Not when my palm retains the stink of some creature's rancid saliva.

Not when I recall that Mikhail would kiss me like that, before biting my flesh hard, because after pleasure, all that remains is to experience pain.

Not when I recognize in my palm the dead stench of the rat that awaits me, erect in my dreams.

Vlahutza watches me lean overboard, vomiting a yellow fear that is lost in the waters of the Bosphorus.

I I

I FEEL IT slide over me, without haste, with a majestic slowness. I am conquered territory, the skin of my neck shuddering at the feel of whatever it is that grazes the base of my throat, gliding quickly over my chest, touching it with absolute freedom.

I open my eyes without knowing where I am, who I am. I see the ceiling, can feel the heat of the sun on the wood. The weight of heat on the bridge.

Objects that I have not secured drift across surfaces, whispering as they slide.

Muffled by distance, the mast thrums as it cuts the air. Easy to imagine the swollen sails.

There are no clothes on my body; at some point during my dream, I must have pulled free of them without realizing it.

I touch my skin and something more.

I look at the tips of my fingers, wet.

That awakened me: the feeling of sweat as it slowly seeped from my pores, leaving its path of salt on my body.

Liquid skin, living oil.

We have left the route of ice, until we cross the Bay of Biscay, a couple of days from England and the end of our trip.

Meanwhile, we are in the heat, the dry breeze that clings to our flesh. No more icy mists or gray seas. Under us lies the green and the slow evaporation of the waters.

Coats will be piled up willy-nilly. Clothes will be left open, gaps for breeze and sweat.

Gaps for my eyes, to guess the hidden forms, the occult secret of muscles and desire.

I have slept no more than a couple of hours. But what does it matter if the sun is out?

I dress and go out to the bridge, to the shouts of the First Mate ordering men to survey the knots in the shroud of the main mast.

I can see my men climbing hand over fist, their bare feet anchored in the rigging, which digs into the edges of their heels, whitened by the grip of their toes, a perfect vision of taut muscles.

Vlahutza has also taken off his shoes. Why not? This is our first day of real heat, of new sweat. The beginning of dry lips, sunburned eyelids, and acid sores that will refuse to close, skin afire, but what does it matter right now?

The wind is strong and we can feel the determined momentum of the schooner. All ship surfaces, despite the breeze, are hot. If one rakes one's hand through one's hair, one will discover there a feverish shimmer, as if each strand were a loaf of bread fresh from the oven.

Were it not for the humid atmosphere that surrounds us, the heavy mantle of invisible salt and water from which it is impossible to escape, it would not be difficult to imagine ships burning in the dark, riggings full of flame. Embers lending slight illumination to the darkness of the aftermath, smoke an offering to the sun's unbridled power.

The uniforms of the men guarding the Straits of the Dardanelles gape open and they are thankful for the shade of canvas.

The customs *felucca* maneuvers toward us. Their swain well knows how to draw more speed from the continuous wind, so we have no need to furl any sails.

The functionaries of the Bosphorus must have telegraphed ahead, revealing how easy it is to get more money from us.

Vlahutza attends to them. I know he will pay the taxes and the bribe with a firm gesture. He will not haggle, nor add some extra coins.

Today, I am off duty. I shall greet the Captain of the Guard, and watch his dark skin glow with sun and sweat.

I lean against the gunwale while they climb the ladder. My men work without excessive effort.

Petrofsky has trouble hoisting a tarp. It is no great weight, but he appears exhausted. His torpid movements give the impression that he feels sick. Without realizing it, as one might push one's hair away from one's forehead, he puts his hand to his neck.

I approach him, look up, and I can see traces of exhaustion on his face, dark circles around his eyes, dregs of white nights.

Petrofsky stands still before me with an indolent gesture. I am another inconvenience of a hard day.

I touch his chin with a firm, abrupt gesture. He is one of my men, so this is no caress; I just let my fingers slide toward the jaw hinge, over his sweaty skin. I turn his head, revealing his neck.

An irregular red spot stands out on his flesh.

I still remember how Mikhail would cling to my chest, how I should shiver when his lips wrapped around my nipple, the wet tongue, then the pull when he sucked my flesh with all his might, his cheeks hollowing, his cravings manifest on my skin. What remained was that dark trace where his mouth had not settled, the space between his lips, an imperfect circle, ellipse of dead blood under the skin, a clear sign of the moment in which pain and excitement are one.

Acketz, at the helm, looks at me. When Melih's men were on board, he did not leave Petrofsky's side.

There is nothing to say, no relevant order.

Vlahutza might have beat him, leaving fresh blood in various other spots. Or he would have burdened him with more tasks, a punishment for the pleasure no sailor should receive if it interferes with his work.

All I can do is order him to go to sleep for a few hours.

I know I am going to think about that stain, the precise drawing made during pleasure, whether I could put my lips around that cryptic glyph ....

The Turks are already on board. They inspect the sails as if they were looking for something printed on them, but it is not the labyrinth of cables and canvas that attracts their attention. It is easy to guess by their gestures that they search for the source of some smell they dislike.

No schooner is fragrant. The wood rots. The sails mildew. Copper plates slowly corrode, giving off an aroma of dust and iron, of rusty sea. Not to mention the cargo that has spoiled below, a stench that hangs over the hold, lingering above the boxes we transport to England.

Mayhap it is that: the odor of black earth in the midst of the sea.

Forest on board, full of dead leaves, fungi and blind worms, of albino life developing hidden from view in the eternal night of the hold.

If there is now an unpleasant stink aboard the *Demeter,* it has invaded so gradually that there is no way to know how or when.

The customs officers' work is thorough, counting the boxes and checking our papers, but with great celerity. They want us out of their straits as soon as possible. They do not want our boat in those waters once night falls.

In Russia, we dream of wolves in the midst of the forest. What image does that black earth awaken in the Turks?

I2

A SOUND. A small splash in the water.

I watch a gray rat run across the deck. Its skin hangs loose on its bones; it has spent so much time hiding that it has not eaten in days.

Quickly, it climbs the wood, scurrying down the bowsprit without stopping. It looks at the *felucca* that bobs a few yards from the *Demeter*. It jumps without thinking. Another splash. Faint churning of little limbs. Above the persistent thrum of the sea, it is nigh-on imperceptible unless one knows what is happening. But I do. I saw that first rat rush, guilty, toward the water and the ship that could whisk it away from a certain death.

Falling bodies, tiny shipwrecks.

Even when they fall no more, I keep hearing them.

A Turkish officer looks at the *Demeter*, then at the rats that swim toward his boat. He whispers some words I cannot hear and steers away, toward the coast.

We will go out to the Aegean Sea in a couple of hours, when it gets dark.

I LOOK AT the deckhead above me. Dark wood pitted by the salt of a thousand trips, witness of many routes and captains. From my cot, I cannot reach the ceiling. Far from my hands, the boards cleave close to one another without any ornamentation. They are utilitarian. As serious as those joined to make coffins for peasants, in *mujik* burials that deliver the dead to that earth from which they drew their lives. Rough boxes, without personality or detail, whose purpose is found in the hidden spaces of dissolution.

It is bootless to think of my room as a coffin.

And it goes without saying that the last vision of those buried alive, just before asphyxiation, are those same slats suspended above them.

I cannot stop smiling.

The point of staying awake is to avoid my nightmares, to avoid Mikhail waiting under the sheets. Why, then, do I lie here thinking about the secret runes of wood that only the dead can decipher?

I get on my feet, repeating that it is logical that coffins be coarse, rough. If you awaken in your grave, you will need to hold on to *something*.

What are these morbid thoughts compared to what I fear I shall find in my dreams?

Mayhap there is something worse than the nothing to which we deliver the dead, than the heavy mantle of earth with which we drape their rotting forms.

The worst part is that they may not be alone down there.

How about *that* intimation to help one forget one's nightmares, eh?

I laugh, thinking about some black *thing* knocking on the rough wood as if it were a door.

Knock, knock.

I hug, feeling myself shiver.

"Who is it?"

If Vlahutza has left the bridge to ask me why I am laughing myself to death, I could answer, honestly: It matters not what that hidden *thing* might answer underground. The loneliness of the grave is so vast that one would open regardless of the cost of that company.

Better than sleeping every night with an oneiric rat beneath the sheets.

Its disgustingly human hands touching my sex, its sickly fur pressing against my body, its twitching bald tail curling around my legs, slipping inside me.

Its black lips, full of insects and rot, pressing against my lips ....

And the fundamental fact that I am as hungry for those lips as they are for mine.

Isn't it better to knock on wood, even that of one's own coffin?

I cannot stop laughing. Not until I realize that someone is watching me.

A rat in a corner of the room.

My laughter fades till the cabin is silent. I stare at the animal without daring to do anything else.

A ship rat, gray and hairy, all wiry muscle beneath that dirty pelt. It does not move. Yet *something* shudders inside its flesh, its throbbing gristle.

It watches me with small, reddish eyes. I am also still. The way it runs its eyes over me makes it clear that I am not of interest. Just another object in the cabin, a piece of furniture casually endowed with voice, but nothing more.

It turns its head toward the entrance. Something there has caught its attention.

Its hair bristles slowly. The rat seems to grow, or mayhap each bristle of hair rises to hide the rat inside. It bares its teeth like a dog, spits a threat at something I cannot see, something out of sight in the corridor. It backs up without ceasing to growl, ready to attack if anything pounces on it. There is no escape, only one corner. It stays there, too scared to understand that it has cornered itself. It does not seem to care. Still it shrinks away, a throbbing mass of fear. Its growling is no longer a threat, not the whistling sound they make when we shoo them from bags of seed. It moans like when their backs are broken and they are nothing but sheer pain twisting and squirming till death overcomes them.

But this rat is unharmed. There is nothing on it that suggests injury or illness.

It frightens me not. How to fear something that is itself so afraid?

But it looks with such fear at the open door that I feel obliged to discover what awaits in the corridor.

It is not the wisest course of action, yet I cannot resist. I must check. I tell myself that mayhap I should grab my pistol, call the Second Mate.

I look out the door, ready for everything.

But there is nothing.

Or nearly nothing.

Something runs in the dark, small claws scratching the floor. A tiny figure flees in the shadows, a white and imprecise blur.

Another rat. An albino rat.

I enter my cabin again and the rat that has sought refuge there stares at me. I want to shrug and inform it that it can relax.

I lie down and reassure myself that the ship rat will also stay awake, afraid of dreams.

14

THE WOOD IS *warm, as if keeping the memory of the sun inside. I can feel it under my bare feet, the rough skin that I tread, the sensations on soles that boast almost no sensitivity and yet could sketch out, if I desired, the lines and contours of the boards. Tree sand on this beach built for us.*

On the other hand, the cold on my skin is nearly liquid. I have no clothes to keep it at bay, so it runs its avid tongue over my flesh, swirling it lightly where there is more warmth: my cheeks, my armpits, my groin, my tumescent sex.

Mikhail is in the forecastle, waiting for me naked under the sheets, and I go to him.

Sails slap the night with a dry, tight snap. I can see red veins on the cloth, stretched, filling with blood, like my sex.

The ship is alive. I can feel it in this moment. Blood and wood, shaking against the onslaught, vibrating as the wind penetrates. Like me, she is headed somewhere. The wait makes her tremble in anticipation of pleasure.

I touch the lines that restrain her desire, the ones that link ship to sails. It feels as though someone, something, were touching the root of my cock, the insensitive base of the beginning. But as that prepuce covers my sex, what I see of the **Demeter** *is nothing more than skin that must be pulled aside, moistened so it can separate more easily.*

What wets me is not spindrift, not spray on the breeze. Upon my skin and the ship pools the slow humidity of before.

It readies itself.

Mikhail is also waiting.

What makes me shudder is not his warm lips, his thin fingers, or the naked sex that seeks me out.

What caresses me is the distance, the space between us, whether far or near.

His skin is not as important as the thought of that skin. The taste I yearn for now, without having yet tasted it, the shudder of semen that still remains within him.

It is the man who has not yet probed my lips with his tongue, but who I can guess in the meantime is the cold that sips my breath.

I can see neither sea nor stars. A mist rises from the waters, from inside the ship. This is right, just. Neither the schooner nor I are here in the present moment, but in that which is to come.

When Mikhail arrived at the house, when I first explored a space in search of him, I remember the dark snow on the other side of the windows. Night snow, white darkness.

Mist.

There is no one on the bridge, no man at the helm. The snow hides them. They have taken refuge next to the fire to survive the winter.

I cannot allow this.

I am the Captain. Although Mikhail is there, caressing himself, I am responsible for this ship.

Who could have told me that I should one day postpone pleasure, desire, for duty?

Not even I.

Or mayhap I could have. I have exchanged my duty for guilt, because I know what happened to Mikhail, the reason he rests in a **mujik** grave, far from consecrated ground.

I take the helm. My hands close firmly on the wheel. The wood is warm but not from the sun. There is no sun in the mist, in the dark snowfall.

The wood is soft. I can sink my fingers into it slightly, softened as it is by a thousand hands that have touched it before. Our course is important.

As though simply wishing it suffices, I remove the mist from me, leaving a path between the stars and the instruments. I measure the angle of elevation, verify the figures *against the nautical calendar. All this without leaving the helm, while I point the* **Demeter** *back in the right direction.*

She shudders, suddenly heavy. The sails momentarily lose their stiffness. Men should trim them, catch the wind again. But I am alone with the helm that groans under my hands. No wooden voice, just effort creaking inside. The wheel groans and I understand.

Without releasing it, I penetrate its center, allowing my foreskin to retract, the wood to encompass my sex. There is no humidity and yet it is easy to enter the **Demeter***, which directs her bowsprit in the right direction, toward England.*

The sphincter of the helm is the right size for my sex, but I can sense its strength. If it should close tightly enough, it could rip my cock away, but the ship wants me to stay inside, to feel her, vibrating with the wind, that continual whisper over the waves, liquid and dry in a thousand parts. I do not move. There is no need. The ship moves for me, ramming the waves, burying its rudder in the waters and its main mast in the night. The lines vibrate, transmitting the sensations to my glans, each piece a part of me, and I can feel everything, muscles of cloth, tree, cable, wind and water.

Slowly, I deliberately turn the helm. I spin the wheel around my sex.

The rudder, the reckoning, the route.

Penetrating it, clinging to the helm, while I speak to someone standing behind me, I don't know whether naked or clothed, erect or watching.

It matters not.

Nothing does: not Mikhail, not the fact, gleaned from my breathing, that I am about to ejaculate inside my ship.

What will be the schooner's reaction?

I can feel the man (someone, something) behind me, smiling, while I shudder.

I know he is satisfied with my pleasure, as though he has granted me the **Demeter** *in exchange for the rat under the sheets.*

Mayhap he has, and so can see me with eyes full of night, while I fear him not.

Why should I do so in the quiet lassitude of after?

In some fashion that I cannot ken, I have made a pact with him.

The man behind me listens. I mutter words that might be related to navigation, but little do they matter.

Not in the dream.

For a moment, I can set aside the images and perceive reality. My cabin and my hand firmly closed on my cock, caressing it.

I return to the vision, continue enjoying the **Demeter**.

But even there, in the midst of intense pleasure, comes the unbroken shriek of a rat.

Cornered, screaming before a dry and definitive click silences his voice.

15

Vlahutza studies the stars with the sextant and carefully reviews the nautical almanac to calculate our position. A task I carried out hours before and whose results he consults, making his own dead reckoning, to certify that his captain is not sending the *Demeter* into the abyss.

We have rounded the Cape of Matapan and the waters are calm. No surprises await in their currents or in the slow rhythm of the waves. The Messenian Gulf offers us the same tranquility that must exist in its depths.

The same illusory aspect as fragile ice ready to break under our feet.

And in order not to hear the lure of that spellbinding liquid, the promised peace awaiting us, motionless, the First Mate seeks order in the constellations, the position and distance that separate us from the end of our route: the port awaiting us in England.

At this moment, that distant border makes little sense, much like the hawsers that we will use to moor the schooner quayside.

The only certain thing is those stars that have not changed in generations, the imperturbable rhythm of the stopwatch, the magnetic compass that does not rest, the figures on our tide charts, the shipwrecks written down in logbooks full of salt that we rescue so that they point out the sites hidden, the other abysses located in the abyss of the sea.

The First Mate does well to anchor us in this world with the numbers written down in the logbook, the longitude and latitude that the *Demeter* occupies.

We are not in the middle of nowhere. We are en route. We know where we are going.

The men who walk along the deck, throwing some debris overboard, securing lines, repairing canvas, believe they have crossed the invisible routes so often that they know them beforehand. But they and I should be helpless without the markings on the maps, without the declensions noted in the almanac, without the naviga-

tion charts carefully transcribed by men who—mayhap—
do not know the sea.

There must always be at least two men on each ship
who can calculate the course, who know the weak secrets
of navigation. Vlahutza and I know that each of us is here
in case the other dies. We are continuations of truncated
destinies, descendants of he who dies in the hypothetical catastrophe. Ghosts of each other.

Petrofsky also looks like a ghost up there, scrutiniz-
ing something high up in the rigging. We all regard him
as though what he does is especially dangerous, but no
blow of the wind, no movement of the *Demeter* justifies
that apprehension in someone who daily trims the sails
and secures the lines.

Something has changed since the darkness fell, as if we
heard the world freezing rapidly around us, surrounded
by the terrible *rassol* of the Bothnian Sea, salt ice forming
needles in the white mantle that yearns to imprison ships.

The crew is dissatisfied with something, scared, but
they refuse to talk, mayhap because their fears are formless and vague.

There are no signs of coming rain and, nevertheless,
we regard the sky. Waiting for the water to drop upon us
and dissolve our restlessness.

And here we are, salty dogs, veterans of a thousand
trips, yearning for a storm to calm us.

16

"THERE ARE NO rats, sir," says Arghezi, while leaving the food on the table.

I regard him, not knowing what expression my face might bear.

"Not enough," he clarifies.

"Enough for what?" Muresh interrupts, but I already know.

"Didst check the storerooms well?" I ask, without letting fear weigh on my words.

"Yes, Captain. They have not infested the provisions."

"Everything is normal?"

"Everything, sir."

That is to say, there were the common traces of their activity: droppings mixed with food, but no nest there, no white pups twisting in the flour.

It is the ninth day of navigation. With no more cargo than the boxes of earth, the rats should have left their hiding places in search of something to eat.

Normally, they would have reached our cabins looking for crumbs, clearing a path between our food and their hunger.

It is true that in the thousand corners that exist in every ship, in the depths of the dead work of the *Demeter*, there must be enough garbage and debris to keep our rat crew alive for days, but they always prefer fresh food, whether to bother us or to make us feel their disdainful supremacy. When they run up to the deck and climb with obese precision along the ropes and masts, they seem to tell us that they are the true owners of our ship. We sail to maintain them. We cross great distances and seven seas to provide them exotic food, delicacies from around the world. They do not hide.

Not without reason.

Nine days is not much time. No reason to scare the crew by asking about rats. Mayhap they have just been hiding, chewing through some unknown delicacy.

Or perhaps not.

"Muresh, go fetch me the First Mate."

Muresh looks at the Cook. The appropriate thing is that someone of lower rank must comply with these types of orders. His expression tells me that he does not consider it *fair* that I should send him. I suspect he spends too much time with Vlahutza. However, he still goes.

"Has anyone reported sick?" I ask the Cook.

"No, sir."

"Dost know what to look for?"

"Aye, sir. Sore throat, lumps of dense flesh in the armpits and groin. Nodules on the neck. Fever."

The symptoms of plague.

I remember my father telling me about the eclipse of rats, waning rats while the disease incubates inside the streets. Black rats that nobody sees again. After their disappearance, the deaths begin. Then the fires in the streets, the heavy wagons carrying the dead and rags that look the same in the dark.

We know of the plagues in India, of a thousand dead in a pyre that never ceases its burning, while elephant gods are begged for the return of rats and normalcy.

"Captain?"

Vlahutza and Muresh enter the cabin, crowding it further. Nigh-on half of the crew present.

The Cook and I shall not mention diseases and rodents. I know I shall not write anything in the logbook. Not until someone finds the small bodies and touches one of the dying animals to certify that in its fatty flesh there are livid nodules, hard as wood. Then I shall lower the sails and let fly the white flag that will prohibit us from entering any port, make us await some solution at sea.

I order Vlahutza to put fewer men on duty. Let the crew rest today as much as possible. Tomorrow, they must redistribute the cargo, find new positions for the boxes of earth.

The First Mate listens to me, saying nothing. Extra meaningless work, shouts and orders to a crew that already has enough dealing with the daily routine.

"I don't see why we should move the cargo," he says.

It is not a challenge. It does not oppose my orders. It simply lists a sufficient fact. The tone of his voice does not allow one to guess, but it seems that he is about to shout his protest, to refuse to obey. The Second Mate and the Cook prepare for another demonstration of Vlahutza's bad humor. But I know him. He is simply telling the crew, telling himself, that he will not be as bad a captain as I. That he will never move cargo in the middle of a journey, or if he does, he will order it in such a way that no one can mumble under his breath (as he does) concerning the merits of his superior.

"Start tomorrow, during Arghezi's watch," I say, acting as though it just occurred to me, as one more way to bother him. "Ye may all of you withdraw."

Upon the table, the food. Once I am alone, I chew it without noticing its flavor, too focused am I upon the movement of my face when biting, upon the muscles of my neck ....

MIKHAIL, IN MOMENTS of calm, with sweat drying on our bodies, liked to speak to me in a low voice, as though sharing the only story he had learned in his life were something more intimate than intercourse.

Caresses on my flesh, the delicate taste of his skin, and his voice: *'A pilgrim who was going to India met a woman with white clothes and black lips. 'Who or what are you?' he asked. 'I am the Plague and I go to India, where I shall kill a thousand men.' On the return trip, the pilgrim met the woman again. 'Why did you lie to me? I went to India and a thousand men had not died: There were ten thousand victims and the pyres have not stopped burning.' 'I told you the truth,' said the Plague. 'I killed only a thousand; the others died of fear.'"*

"They must not see us," he whispered furiously in my ear. "No one can know. Fear can cause ten thousand to die and it can make ten thousand kill, as well."

"Fear of what?"

He touched my cock lightly with his mouth, his saliva and my spilled semen mingling, an imprecise border that ended only in caressing skin, lips gently pressing.

He looked up at me, far away, on the other side of the flesh.

"Fear of us."

18

I TURN TO the dead work, to the sound of the sea below decks, the whisper of the depths that the *Demeter*'s hull barely tastes. The wood ignores the copper plates that cover it. Alone, it knows the secret currents, the incessant slicing of liquid.

The sea is calm, heave and sway nigh-on imperceptible. I sling my lamp to the deckhead and watch its movement, as though a secret breeze plays with it, causing a thousand liquid shadows to dance throughout the space.

It is nearly possible to believe that the hold has been flooded by a sea of shadows.

And there are fish in its waters.

Living beings that travel the depths of my ship; crackling fish of dry fins, whispery anemones; fabrics and objects, wood and ropes tensing and sliding with the heave and sway. A haunted house with myriad ghosts. Revenants we have known so many years that we now require them. There is no silence on the route, nor any way of closing one's senses to the movement.

Were it possible to hear the silence of nothing, it would not be necessary for the crew to move the cargo tomorrow, unwittingly startling the rats with the task, discovering by accident their nests and hiding places. Then Arghezi should not need to be present, looking for them, scouring the shadows in search of bodies.

I stop here, breath shallow so that the air I inhale makes little noise, as though it were possible to distinguish between the diverse sounds of the *Demeter*.

Sometimes, it was possible to hear, in the house of my parents, the ceaseless groan of the wind, the crunching weight of the snow bearing down on the roof, the sandy spray of snowfall against the windows.

The *Demeter* is the same, a home alive in the midst of the elements. Here as well, in the momentary calm where silence does not exist, I should be able to distinguish the continuous gnawing of rats, a scrabbling hint of what hides between the walls.

I remember that constant, meticulous animal creak. A rhythm in that endless sound.

When I was but another sailor, I listened a thousand times, in the dark, to some fellow crewman masturbating. Furtive sounds, like the scampering of rats. Insistent, precise. A rhythm also in them.

A rhythm different from mine.

Nervous, fast. As though they wished to hurry to climax. Ejaculate into their palms and finally find sleep.

At such moments, I also touched my sex, masturbating as silently as possible, imagining the semen would seep into my clothes or the rough cloth on which we slept, liquids drying in the gathered heat.

I thought then, like now, about rats.

Did they also expect some of that thick liquid to fall? Did they, like me, hope to taste its harsh tang?

Would they sip it carefully?

If those drops fell, would the rats bury their teeth in the wood of the floor? Would they extend thin tongues to drink up every drop?

It became a matter of keeping my semen from the rats. I tried not to let any drops escape my palm, bringing my face close to the warm scent. I drank it slowly. A dense taste, with the feverish temperature of my sex, bloated with blood.

I think of Muresh, the warm food I serve him.

Would any of my men who happened to descend at this moment understand why his captain slowly masturbates in the hold? Would he understand the care with which I drip my semen onto the wood?

Does the invitation stir rats that may no longer exist?

19

"Captain."

The voice of Arghezi, somehow in the midst of my dream, although in this one, only the *Demeter* and I remain, sharing the vague pleasure of ramming the waves.

I open my eyes and see the Cook's face above me, while he shakes me lightly. A movement would suffice and I could sip his breath, touch his lips with my tongue.

"Captain."

A whispering, intimate voice. He wants no one to hear. I want him closer. I can feel the heat of Arghezi's skin.

Fever.

I remember then and awaken immediately, scrabbling away from that feverish face, from the disease that has reached my bed.

Arghezi has to grab me, keep me from falling to the floor.

"Wake up, sir."

When he touches me, I know he is real. The temperature of our skins is identical. Both safe from the plague, or already dying.

"What is it?"

Before he answers, the possibilities are already all-but certain. Who has fallen? What shall I do then?

"You *must* accompany me," he says.

I dress in silence, while the Cook turns his eyes toward the dark corridor. Shoulders raised, head slightly tilted forward, hands touching his forearms, he hides his chest in an innervated hug.

He seems a man in the midst of an ice storm, with no more protection than his own flesh. The only certainty is that skin, the unbroken flow of blood.

But it is not the cold that makes his lips tremble.

He has *seen* something; something has happened that makes him retreat into a corner, ready to groan like a rat.

Something he wants to show me.

We cross the deck without saying a word, without calling out to any of the men who work the last watch of the day. I look at the canvas, dry skin hanging on a wooden skeleton. Arghezi points to the hold. Where else? I do not want to go, not to the place where the Cook refuses to return. Whatever scared him is there ….

But I am the Captain and someone must do it.

The hold is full of fog, coiled tight against the floor, flowing fast and easy, tides of mist in a white sea.

It is clear outside, sky and ocean free of haze. I do not imagine a fire, the hold filling with smoke. No. This fog is screaming.

I descend without knowing why. Mayhap I wish to verify that what I see is real, that I am not in another dream from which I shall be awakened by a man who swears my ship has been condemned by the plague.

Arghezi stays above, holding the lamp that casts my shadow on whatever it is that shudders in the darkness.

A sharp, continuous scream, without volume. Secret. Like Arghezi's whisper. Like Mikhail muttering, "Very well." A multiple shout, composed of a hundred different sounds.

I understand it, when I go down into the fog, when something small stirs beneath my foot and sinks its little teeth into my shoe.

A white rat.

Thousands of them on the floor, blurred by their rapid movements. Screaming with an unknown voice, as if their color and hunchbacked bodies distorted their sounds as well. I can hear them, but not the skittering of their nails against the wood, nor the rapid drumming of their steps. They seem not to touch the floor.

A gray rat runs past me, fleeing toward Arghezi, chased by the white ones. He is about to escape but they leap upon him, sharp teeth digging into his entire body.

A territorial fight.

For this reason had they disappeared for ten days: the new ones learning the terrain, the old ones hiding before the superior number of the others, fights in the shadows, deaths and murders behind the studs, under the floors, between the beams.

It is not difficult to guess how the white rats have arrived; they surround the boxes of earth as if determined to protect them. Mayhap their nests lie within.

I lean all my weight onto my foot, crushing the biting rat. It begins to vomit blood, too much for that thin, wiry body.

I want to crush them all, tear each one apart. I know not why. Mayhap that voice, the meaningless screeching they collectively emit, their tiny, blood-colored eyes ….

It becomes a matter of closing the hold. There is insufficient food for such a number. Let them die in the eternal darkness of the dead work; let them eat one another.

That might kill the deep fear they evoke in me, the certainty that I felt, for a moment, that the darkness had not confused me, that before becoming rats, they had been fog that oozed from the boxes of earth, seeping through the tight weft of wood that I know is not wide enough to let anything out ....

20

"SOMETIMES, THEY SCREAM like pigs."

I look up, startled. Olgaren continues to look at the tightly closed hatch of the hold. He does not await an answer, but plays unconsciously with a loop of rope tied to his wrist, three large knots that he rubs with his fingers. It seems a rosary, but is not. Or in any event, the prayers required for it are different. Three knots: If one undoes the first, it releases a moderate wind; the second, a gale; and the third unleashes the gusting voice of a hurricane.

The same Finnish man offered it to me at the port of Hierapetra, after many days of calm. Olgaren bought it because he also believes in the efficacy of sewing small nets to one's clothing to ward off demons. And he assures us that gunpowder mixed with liquor makes him a veritable stallion. *Up to twice in one night,* he usually proclaims with pride that makes the claim impossible to refute. A child still surprised at the miracle of his body.

Now he is a child who has not quite awakened from a bad dream.

"And they stink, Captain. They squeal and blow dead breath from their mouths, as if they'd eaten carrion or were themselves dead inside …."

Joachim and Petrofsky have moved away, weary, it seems, of Olgaren and his stories.

"And they come out only at night. Have ye not marked it? They are white and come out only at night, because white is a sickly color in the dark."

Olgaren wears an open shirt that reveals part of his shoulders. Upon them a bruise fades, losing definition. A blow from Vlahutza at the beginning of the trip. I ask not why: It is easy to guess. When Olgaren feels compelled to say something, he cannot stop; he cannot prevent what has fermented in his mind from coming out.

"But they don't touch us. For some reason, they won't cross our path, nor do they gnaw our things. They haven't come to us. I haven't felt any pattering feet upon my body. Shadows of rats, that's what they are. And they keep to themselves and that should be enough for us, knowing that they'll stay down there. But they shriek like pigs in the dark. The others don't care, 'Let them do what they want as long as they don't bite us,' but I should also have locked them in the hold, same as ye."

Then he realizes his words, what it would have cost him if they had been heard by Vlahutza. That tone of approval, acknowledging that the Captain has done - for once - the right thing. His blessing for the measure taken, for canceling the redistribution of the cargo and ordering, instead, that closed hatch, and the reward of an extra cup of liquor for each white rat found dead on deck.

He looks at me, not knowing what my reaction might be.

"Thank you," I answer, because I am not Vlahutza.

I watch him go, glancing over his shoulder at the sea as if afraid something might emerge from its depths.

The plague was not the *something* that frightens them. Nor was it the absent rats.

The true source of fear falls on me like a persistent rain.

The same gnawing worry shared by Mikhail and me and all who carry our queer appetites like stigmata.

eyes

21

I GO OUT into the night and the wind, into the relative calm of the last watch of the day, with a man working the deck and another at the helm.

I was drowning in my cabin, in the riotous flood of my thoughts. I know that pleasure awaits me in my dreams, as once the rat awaited, but I cannot abandon myself to sleep.

I remember that I abandoned myself to Mikhail and he to me.

He is buried at a crossroads, condemned, according to the men who left him there, never to find peace.

And I, alive, safe, cannot sleep, though pleasure awaits me in the dark.

I think of Petrofsky, of the brand he bears upon his skin, of the moment when flesh ceases to be a border.

I can see the bodies in the warm atmosphere, wet with sweat, fingers eager to slip between the muscles, when the need to tear exceeds mere arousal, a certainty that the body beside us—whether penetrating or penetrated—is ours, and to confirm the truth that there is nothing quite like pain, fingernails digging grooves into backs, the feeling of skin opening, the exquisite shudder that thrums along nerves and infects us, as if the wound were fresh in our own flesh ....

I hear the sea around me, or mayhap blood pounding in my ears. It matters not. I know that I can accompany Petrofsky in the bow.

I make no noise. It is impossible to hear my bare feet on the wood. I also think of my parents' home in Dzerzhinsk, of the nights when I would get up from my bed to wander the dark rooms, understanding that the house was no longer a communal place. In the shadows, once all the doors were closed, private spaces came into being, secrets hidden under sheets, sheltered by the hours of night.

Then, as now, slight spasms of delirium; fear and enjoyment fused and I knew not which caused me to risk opening doors in guilty silence, to peer through the cracks at sleeping forms of those who misused that precious time.

Acketz is asleep on deck, hugging himself, as though even in sleep he must protect himself from something.

Petrofsky is alone.

That excites me. Alone, having already permitted someone to mark his flesh.

Alone like me, at this moment.

Petrofsky stands by the mainstay of the foremast, looking up at the sky, pale and trembling, so absorbed he sees naught but his horror. I follow his gaze, seeking what must hang amongst the cold stars, turning him into a statue of salt.

There are but a pair of clouds that move slowly, barely visible in the glow of the night.

Petrofsky's hair is shaken by the wind, open shirt exposing his white chest, pantaloons clinging to his wiry legs like wet clothes.

Petrofsky seems submerged in a sea of wind, sinking into unknown depths while watching the surface grow farther away, the fading border he has crossed to encounter these insubstantial waters that drown him.

His hands touch his bare chest, run down it. He attempts to convince himself that he is real, that he is awake. I can hear him gasping, looking for something—a scream, a word—that might allow him to understand or express something impossible.

Again, I let my eyes drift upward along the ropes and the tense sails, the insensate design of the rigging, toward the darkness above us.

Only clouds.

Then I understand and I also feel I am drowning in nothing.

The wind has come alive in the canvas. It strives to strip Petrofsky's clothes from his body, giving an audible whine as it penetrates our ears, sensitive pressure.

Yet, the clouds above drift indolently in the opposite direction from the unbridled gale that envelops us.

Clouds moving in another universe, a different night than the one through which we sail. The speed of the *Demeter* leaves them behind, high and delicate, without the least evidence that the wind touches them or drives them as it does us.

I regard the sea, the waves that roughen our travel, the slight veil of foam the wind rips from their crests, its fury reshaping them into titanic surges. Impossible to see whether in the distance, on that black horizon, the sea also roils and roars, or whether yonder waters are so still they reflect the stars.

The wind surrounds Petrofsky, rocking to and fro through his hair, giving him a crazed air. He says something, seems to speak to someone in the midst of that invisible flow, the wind entering his mouth, muddying his voice.

I stand a mere dozen paces from him, but it is as though I were on the other side of the world. The lines grow tense like veins; the sails are muscles about to burst, each billowing in a different direction.

The snapping of the canvas makes a sketch of the formless wind; at its center is Petrofsky.

An invisible hand tousles his clothes, exposes a shoulder, luminous in the night.

He raises a hand, which hovers a few inches from his bare skin, as if something prevents him from touching his own flesh. It seems he rests his palm on nothing.

The wind casts his hair over his face and each strand seems to have a life of its own, twitching along his features, pulling away to leave areas bare, pressing against him to hide his eyes, exposing the sensitive back of his neck.

Then comes the moment when I know I must still be lying in bed, dreaming about insomnia and the deserted bridge, because the wind stops touching me and the *Demeter*. Calm envelops us like a silence, sails and moors hanging lifeless throughout the entire ship.

And then … *I can see the wind.*

Condensing, congealing, first invisible, then tremulous as in the midday heat, next running in rivulets of water, deep currents of frigid sea, clear ice and haze and fog and falling snow, and finally night without light.

And in its midst, Petrofsky, slowly stripped by invisible hands, caressing concrete shadows.

His mouth is open as if to scream, but his tongue licks at something that is not there, his hands cling to nothing, his sex swings free to penetrate no one ....

A dream.

I tell myself that I am in my cabin, sleeping far from reality, and that I only dream the distant, languid moan of the sailor, the heavy panting of pleasure. Answering the wind, surrendering the self for a second, exhaling during the dense satisfaction of orgasm.

22

THE NIGHT NEVER ceases when we wish. I open my eyes to await the sun, the daily awakening routine, Arghezi bringing round the first meal of the day.

Instead, there is the dark sea, the gray wake fading into the distance, the brief and definitive grinding of the helm as it struggles to keep us on course. The wind again.

Olgaren keeps the route, silent.

The full sails are, in their whiteness, like another pale moon in the distance. I look sternward, at the masts of the *Demeter* bearing their heavy rigging. A strange foliage, trees hiding between the bolts of cloth and hemp that surround us.

We ride through nocturnal forests toward another darkness, immersed in the aroma of the hidden earth in the hold. Earth from Wallachia, where tombs are still opened to certify that their dead remain motionless, hands free of bites, of that careful, secret gnawing.

The Wieszcy.

Dead devouring themselves, black teeth finishing off dark flesh. And relatives dying at the same time, while the secret feast is consumed. Flesh of their flesh, food in death.

There are men with the habit of sleeping on the graves, waiting for the world to fall silent, for the night to breathe easy, in order to listen to those who inhabit the coffins, to hear flesh tearing deep in the earth, men who swallow their horror when they hear something, pressing against the abyss that yawns under their bodies, supported and formed by the black earth in which they hide their faces, fearing what can be found there ....

Earth we haul across the sea.

I look at my shadow on the ship's wood, nocturnal shade cast by pallid moon.

I notice then that there are too many shadows on the bridge, crossing one another, gray ones going black where several overlap, traces of multiple wicks that have been lit.

Lamps next to the Helmsman, suspended over the bell, next to the board, illuminating the stairs leading to the bridge, Olgaren's white face that focuses more on that watch fire dispersed widely within glass walls than on the compass.

They serve as our protection against the night, the only manner of ensuring that nothing will leap from the black without our seeing what it is.

Yet ... what if the last gift of light is the sight of something that belongs to naught but the night? What if death is more merciful than the appearance of whatever should come for our flesh?

Still, there is no more protection than fire. The insubstantial, flickering walls form the room in which we hide, the only space we count as ours in the unending mansion of the nocturnal sea.

I stand by the Helmsman, knowing that I am no true company, nothing capable of eroding the fear of the man who moves his lips without ceasing.

Well I know the prayer you mutter, a litany composed of descending numbers: the seconds that remain before dawn.

I know the wherefore of my fear. But not that of the Helmsman. There is naught here that should frighten him, only night, and darkness, and the wind that does not cease, and the fluttering sails, and a white-faced captain emerging from the shadows to say nothing, while he observes the transparent sky of the horizon, seeking that nascent light that is his only surety.

Above us, the sky is losing consistency, as if the night were a huge fish plunging into a midday sea, its dark color fading into the transparent blue.

It dawns, while the darkness leaves in search of other depths.

Together with the stars, the wind disappears. A mist rises from the sea and the sails droop. They are no longer taut skins but tired, weak limbs.

The air no longer moans around us; the aroma of earth is now redolent of salt.

The speed of the *Demeter* decreases, until it all-but stops. There is naught but sea around us, no other men than us.

One can perceive the nothingness that isolates us.

Something has finished. In this calm, it is possible to savor that notion, to feel it in every inch of one's skin.

I behold the sunrise and understand.

Light cannot protect us from everything.

TWO

LOG OF THE *DEMETER*

2 3

I STARE AT the bottle next to me, rigorously prepared for shipwreck.

When we sink, when at last we surrender ourselves to the waters or they claim us, the sea will leave a trail of objects to mark the place where we disappeared: blackened canvas, bits of wood, mayhap, if fortune prevails (and if one can call fortunate that which survives our demise), the brief log that I have placed within the glass, transparent memory edited rigorously at night and during storms, words that I shall not be able to say aloud and in person to the owners of the **Demeter**. *I should like to read again what I have written, to recognize the man who pointed out the horror to me.*

I know he is not me.

Who could be himself when he writes and without knowing the silhouette his words demark? The sickly glow of the facts casts a vague shadow, a specter that cannot be given form because it is not we who create it, and which we call days, facts, **reality**.

So few words for a thousand events.

I also am a specter when I write. It is my shadow— stripped of all that matters—that speaks through ink and paper.

A shipwreck's voice, which—strangely—is not that of shredded canvas, of wood cleaved open like a wound, the echo of those who stopped screaming in the midst of the roiling waters.

It is the voice of the wood creaking softly, of those who whisper before anything happens.

The mere facts, their trivial accumulation.

He is not me, but I am the one who writes with haste and thrusts each sheet in the bottle, not knowing what time remains to me, or whether anyone will ever read those words.

Mayhap it matters not.

Mayhap the closeness of the bottle augurs well. I may chance to seize it in my final moments and drag it with me to the bottom of oblivion.

Then no one will ever know what happened and how I let it happen.

Mayhap my redemption is to silence my own voice (which is not my voice).

I read it written.

What else can I do while I wait for the waters to come for me?

I read the words of a man who wrote without knowing what those dry, short, unrecognizable phrases truly meant for him.

I read to remind myself that it was another voice—another man—to whom the events happened.

16 July

*Mate reported in the morning that one of crew, Petrofsky, was missing. Could not account for it. Took larboard watch eight bells last night; was relieved by Abramoff, but did not go to bunk. Men more downcast than ever. All said [those who dared speak beyond a fearful murmur] they expected something of the kind, but would not say more than there was **something** aboard.*

I dared not tell them that I, too, awaited a death. There is no logic in thinking that mere fear can materialize into a "something" that closes its claws round one of our throats.

Vlahutza got very impatient with them, feared some trouble ahead. He needed more than an absence: How, when did Petrofsky cease to be?

Could an explanation end the fear, diffuse the silhouette of the one who is no longer here?

Who says ghosts must be seen?

Petrofsky is in all the places where he is not found, his silhouette projected throughout the *Demeter*, ready to touch us at any moment.

We look at the sea and understand that—if not found on board—he has gone to rest in the depths of those waters, of that region consecrated to all sailors.

But how vast the watery cemetery whispering beyond the wood? How many tombs press against the boat, yearning to drown us?

Useless question.

How many?

Just this one.

17 July

YESTERDAY, OLGAREN, CAME to my cabin and, in an awestruck way, confided to me that he thought there was a strange man aboard the ship.

He said that, in his watch, he had been sheltering behind the deck-house, as there was a rainstorm, when he saw a tall, thin man, who was not like any of the crew, come up the companionway, go along the deck forward, and disappear.

He followed cautiously, holding his storm-catching skein of rope in his left hand—the only amulet at his disposal apart from the steel of the blade in his right.

He planned to corner the stowaway, an encounter in the midst of wind and night during which one of the two must die.

But when he got to the bows, he found no one and the hatchways were all closed.

Nothing but the sea just beyond the hull.

He was in a panic of superstitious fear and I am afraid the panic may spread.

18 July

THE DESCRIPTION OF the stranger is that of the enemy. Someone alien to us, hidden for unknown purposes. All carry a weapon fitting their fear, matching the magnitude of their might. Joachim has taken out an ax bigger than his arm.

Had they dared in this forest of canvas and ropes, they would have held torches, they would have thrown themselves into a *pogrom* against a single man.

I understood that, if everyone hunted the stranger, it was quite possible that they themselves would become the prey.

Later in the day, I got together the whole crew and told them, as they evidently thought there was someone in the ship, we would search from stem to stern.

No one said what we should do upon finding the stowaway.

No one said it while sharpening his steel.

Vlahutza, angry, said it was folly, that all we had on board were cowards frightened by shadows. He said he would engage to keep them out of trouble with a handspike, for to yield to such foolish ideas would demoralize the men.

Better to yield, however, than to allow fear to ferment.

I let him take the helm, while the rest began a thorough search, all keeping abreast, with lanterns, speaking to one another, sometimes shouting.

A line of beaters, they call it in India, when a group of men advances through the tall grass, making a riotous roar by pounding drums, clanging metal and piping whistles to provoke the tiger into fleeing from the disciplined file that can prevent an escape at either flank.

Of course, before each hunt, someone would comment that, at times, the beaters would stumble upon something worse than a tiger, their brave shouts suddenly cut off. Then a silence would fill the thicket, heavy with spilled blood, and at most, there would come a strangled shout that explained it:

"*Rakshasa!*"

The demon, thirsty for blood, hungry for flesh.

Yet, we were thirsty as well, eager to kill the thing we feared with a sharp blow, to shred uncertainty with our weapons.

We left no corner unsearched. We discovered how vast our little *Demeter* can seem, how many hidden corners she has, how many hiding places abound.

Between the ropes, under the bunks, atop the forecastle ….

We went down to the hold all at once. We surrounded the big wooden boxes, searching for the fugitive.

Once again, he had fled.

We found no one. Nothing faced our fury, which became diluted with every yard that we advanced until dissolving into relief when we reached the last corner and realized that, in some way, we had eliminated not only the possibility of the stowaway, but his very existence.

"He *was* onboard," said Olgaren.

But not anymore.

"He might've jumped," said Acketz. "Might've preferred the waters to a noose."

"Aye, or mayhap he went to join Petrofsky," Vlahutza shouted from the helm.

And why not? Everyone recalled the dark mark of a violent caress on the neck of the missing sailor.

What if he who had left that mark was the killer? He couldn't have got on board without Petrofsky's help. Wouldn't he have weakened over time from hunger, sharing half of his ration with the stowaway?

Mayhap they had fought in the shadows. Perchance pleasure had spawned violence.

I listened to my men and I understood why they joined the two shadows as one: They were twinned by our ignorance, made accomplices because we had seen nothing.

But the search had expelled the stranger: better water as revenge than blood spilled on deck.

The men were much relieved when the search was over. They went back to work cheerfully. Vlahutza scowled, but said nothing.

It took me a while to realize. He was the only one who was still afraid.

Not finding the stranger had terrified him more.

Such strange things are happening that from now on, and until we again reach land, I shall write everything down with care.

22 July

ROUGH WEATHER LAST three days, and all hands busy with sails—no time to be frightened.

At the end of the day, when exhaustion covers us like a heavy mantle and our muscles thrum with the incessant rhythm of a storm pressing against every line along the wood of the ship, it is fair to say that we have forgotten our dread.

Nothing sinister save the dark clouds, the rumble of thunder, the continuous and deep voice of the sea. Vlahutza is cheerful again. The storm is a tangible thing onto which he can hold. He can dilute his concerns by imposing his will on the elements. All that matters to him now is that the *Demeter* not founder and sink.

Oddly enough, harmony reigns. I have praised the men for their work in bad weather.

We have passed Gibraltar and come out through the Straits.

All is well.

24 *July*

THE PREVIOUS ENTRY of the 22nd looks up at me, a mockery of Chinese ink.

There seems some doom over this ship.

Already a hand short, entering on the Bay of Biscay with wild weather ahead, and yet last night, another man lost.

Arghezi has disappeared in the midst of the storm in which we have sailed all these days.

I went to look for him at his post. There was only the black presence of the rain.

I screamed his name and the roar of the waves was all that answered.

I sent the men to look for him and they returned, covered in rain and fear.

"Mayhap a wave swept him overboard," said Acketz.

Mayhap, yet the storm has not made the ship list, nor have the thousand neglected objects tumbled from the deck into the sea.

If Petrofsky was a silent ghost, Arghezi shouts throughout the Demeter, a voice of creaking wood, of sails about to rip, of things that fall and roll from side to side.

The men, as one might expect, are all in a panic of fear. It was grave enough that silence devoured one of their number, but they are more afraid of the storm, of the waters that rise from the depths and search them out.

The crew have sent a round robin, asking to have double watch, as they fear to be alone: four men awake at each turn. Seven of us remain, but the impossibility of their demand does not matter. Not when the wind knocks on our doors, eager to enter.

The First Mate is angry. The calm that the storm gave him was exhausted when he read the petition.

"It'll wear us out, you fools …."

He hurled the paper back at Olgaren, who only backed away. His responsibility ended with the delivery of the document. What we did was up to us.

If there were more blood, it would be on our hands.

What if fear should convince them to take command of the *Demeter*? Two voids, two nothings making their spectral way through the ship might inspire a mutiny.

I fear there will be trouble, as either Vlahutza or the men will do some violence.

25 *July*

OLGAREN CAME BACK to my cabin and left his talisman on the table, that skein of lines that binds the wind.

I look at that rotten hemp, the dark-black fungus that has eaten through the knots that form that pagan hex.

I understand.

The amulet has been undone.

The storm has released itself.

28 July

FOUR DAYS IN hell, knocking about in a sort of maelstrom, the wind a tempest.

Four days during which we discover how fear can be devoured by exhaustion, that to be scared one needs an energy we lack.

The storm took care of the signed petition: We have all had to work regardless of schedules. Who can think of watches when the mast groans, near breaking, and the lines in the rigging unravel before the gusting wind and the water licks our ankles, reminding us that it has embarked with us?

Nine men on a ship is not an arbitrary number. We fully understand this arithmetic now that we are only seven.

No sleep for anyone.

It cannot be called sleeping when, for a couple of hours, we practically faint in a dream full of open sea, showing its obscene interior of sunken ships and drowned sailors.

We are all worn out.

We have met, for minutes at a time, attempting to remember how to tie a knot, drowsiness eating our thoughts.

The limit has been reached. I hardly know how to set a watch, since no one is fit to go on.

It is time to secure everything, to lower the sails, to tie down our cargo, and go to sleep without knowing whether we shall wake up at the bottom of the ocean or not.

It is time to surrender to the mercy of something that, we know well, has never had mercy.

Muresh has volunteered to steer and watch.

Watch what?

The dark waves, the wild wind, the clouds falling in sheets upon us, the incessant fog.

Still, I understand: A sailor at the helm means we have not given up completely. A hope, if a man alone in the midst of the sea can rightly be considered hope.

I could have kissed him, but—desire also requires energy.

The rest of us shall sleep for four hours.

We risk life for it, but what more can be done?

I write this down in haste and tell myself (lying is at times necessary) that the wind is abating.

The seas still surge terrifically, but I feel them less.

The ship is steadier.

29 July

THE SILENCE AWAKENED me.

The storm has vanished, leaving a still sea below and an icy sun above.

The men work to repair everything broken, to bail the water, to patch the sails.

They will sleep a long and dreamless sleep tonight.

Muresh and Abranoff will take over at dark. Too exhausted to rejoice, we simply await the coming of evening.

We rest, let our minds wander without any fixed course.

We tell ourselves, with the satisfied tiredness of one who has barely escaped his grasp, that Death merely brushed us with a bony hand before he left.

But it is not true. He has not left.

Another tragedy.

Joachim's shout at an indeterminate hour of darkness.

Single watch tonight, as crew too tired to double. When he came on deck to keep the morning watch, Joachim found only Abranoff at the helm. Muresh, who shared the watch, was missing. He had gone to investigate something at the other end of the ship,

steps

but had never returned.

Raised outcry and all came on deck. We conducted a thorough search, but no one was found. We are now without a Second Mate and crew in a panic.

There is no stranger on board or storm to blame for the disappearance.

There is only the certainty that Muresh was alone when *it* happened, whatever *it* was.

No longer an accident: a purpose.

Vlahutza and I have loaded the guns, slipped blades into our belts. We shall go armed henceforth and wait for any sign of cause.

30 July

THE LAST NIGHT. Rejoiced we are nearing England. Weather fine, all sails set. I retired, worn out. Slept soundly. Vlahutza has awakened me, saying that Acketz and Joachim are missing. Helm was free for many hours, in the dark, and we are now off course.

Now, only Olgaren, Abranoff, Vlahutza, and I remain to work the ship.

1 *August*

Two days of continuous fog, a nothing that devours the sea, the stars, the coasts that might tell us where we are.

I look at the navigation charts, dead paper with vague figures.

The fog surrounds the ship like a shroud, reminding us that we are expelled from the outside world.

Not a sail sighted. No way of knowing whether we have entered the English Channel or have passed it by, heading toward a destination we will never reach. No one to whom we might send a desperate signal.

Not having power to work sails, we watch the canvas swell with air and humidity above us. We have given the helm of the *Demeter* to the wind and the sea, which—needless to say—seem to be against us.

I dare not lower the sails, as we could not raise them again.

We seem to be drifting to some terrible doom.

Vlahutza is more demoralized than all of us.

He cannot impose his rank on the missing.

He regards the ropes with indifference, no longer searches the fog for a hole to use the sextant.

He does not care. Not about the fate of wood.

He has not set his weapons aside even once, but the fog cannot be sliced with a blade and drift is impossible to shoot.

But something living ….

What, in all this misty waste?

His stronger nature seems to have worked inwardly against himself. The men are beyond fear, working stolidly and patiently, with minds made up to the worst. They are Russian, he Romanian.

2 *August*

A CRY.

Not part of the dream, seemingly outside my port. A cry of pain.

Nothing could be seen, with the fog.

I have rushed on deck, not knowing where to run. Vlahutza shouted at me from an alcove lit by lamps, Olgaren's shelter against the night.

There was naught left but a cigar, still smoking, a void whose silence screams.

We watched the ember until it went out.

Abranoff looked down at his own cigar and then hurried to throw it overboard, as if it were an incandescent eye that suddenly winked at him.

One more gone. Lord help us!

Vlahutza says we must be past the Straits of Dover, as in a moment of fog lifting, he saw North Foreland, just as he heard Olgaren cry out.

If so, we are still en route, though now sailing aimlessly through the North Sea. Only God can guide us in the fog, which seems to move with us, and God , it seems, has deserted us.

3 *August*

AT MIDNIGHT, I went to relieve Abranoff at the wheel. When I got to it, I found no one there.

The wind was steady and, as we ran before it, there was no yawing. Any attempt to change course might rip the rigging free, make us list in the water.

I dared not leave the helm, so I shouted for Vlahutza. After a few seconds, he rushed up on deck in his flannels, indifferent to the fierce, icy drizzle that whipped us.

He looked wild-eyed and haggard. He glanced down at the deck and then at me, and I realized he saw shadows that I could not.

Though he saw me struggle with the helm, he did not rush to my aid, but climbed slowly, carefully up the rungs to where I stood, pulling a huge knife out from his flannels.

He slid up behind me.

I couldn't see him. All I could do was wait for …

the blade ….

And I felt his breath for a second sliding down my neck, reaching my ear.

I clearly felt his deep breathing, the warmth of his mouth, brushing my flesh.

He whispered hoarsely, with his mouth to my ear:

"It is here."

Not a gesture of love, but of terror. He feared the very air might hear.

"I know it, now. On the watch last night, I saw It, like a man, tall and thin, and ghastly pale, lit by the sickly glow of mushrooms. It was in the bows, looking out. It made a gesture and the fog dissolved at Its command. I could see the stars above us. I saw It move Its lips (swollen, red), which twisted as It muttered some obscure spell. I crept behind It, as I have behind thee, and gave It my knife."

His voice vibrated, falling and rising in tone, from a hoarse whisper to nigh-on a girlish scream: His reason had given way.

"Dost thou see this blade? Dost thou? Should I bury it in thine eye … dost think thou couldst feel how cold it is in the midst of thy living blood? I always believed it so. I believed in the voice of steel ... yet it failed me. I do not know how. I gave It my steel, I tell thee, but the knife went through It, empty as the air."

And as he spoke, he took his knife and drove it savagely into space. I felt a sudden burn and blood slid down my cheek. He had just cut me without knowing.

And, with a warning look and his finger on his lip, he went below.

"I know where It hides."

He started laughing.

"What is not normal aboard this ship?" he asked.

you

"The cargo, the damned boxes of earth in the hold, savvy? It must hide in one of them. One of the covers must be false. I'll unscrew them one by one and see. Work thou the helm."

He peeked over my shoulder, then touched my lips with his feverish fingers, giving me a warning look.

"Shhh."

He went below. I saw him come out on deck again with a tool chest and a lantern, and go down the forward hatchway.

He is mad; stark, raving mad, and there is no use in my trying to stop him.

What damage can he do to the cargo? Nothing could matter less than the clay we transport.

I can only trust in God and wait till the fog clears. Then, if I can't steer to any harbor with the wind that is, I shall cut down sails and lie by, and signal for help ....

Thus was I thinking when Vlahutza screamed.

Lord, may I never hear another man scream again!

Not like Vlahutza, not like Mikhail.

My blood froze and I was about to go to his aid.

But the hatchway burst open and up on the deck he came as if shot from a gun—a raging madman, with his eyes rolling and his face convulsed with fear. I could see he had pissed himself.

"Save me!" he cried. "Save me!"

He looked round on the blanket of fog. His horror turned to despair. And all of a sudden, he was once more simply Vlahutza. He saw me standing there, alone and terrified, pathetically clutching the wheel.

Whom could I have saved?

"Come with me," he said in a steady voice, a sane man for the last time. "You had better come, too, Captain, before it is too late. He is there. I know the secret now. The sea will save me from Him, and it is all that is left!"

Before I could say a word, or move forward to seize him, he sprang onto the bulwark and deliberately threw himself into the sea, shouting as he condemned himself to exploding lungs and endless suffocation.

Without hesitation, he chose the black face of the drowned, a mouth unhinged by despair, hands that tear bloody grooves in a throat closed forever by the sea.

He jumped toward that end, eagerly.

I suppose I know the secret, now, too.

It was this madman who had got rid of the men one by one, and now he has followed them himself. God help me!

How am I to account for all these horrors when I get to port?

When I get to port!

Will that ever be?

THREE

VOICES LIKE DUST

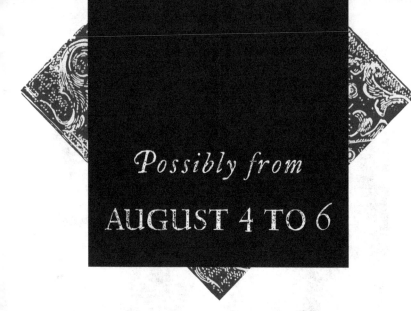

Voices like dust, covering everything, hiding the immutability of the world.

I am at the helm of a dead ship.

What does it matter?

The voices are alive, surrounding me as my men once did. Voices that belong to me, that I shall not write down in the log of the *Demeter* that, now inside the bottle, has ceased to belong to me.

How might it be useful to whoever separates salt from those pages that I speak of Olgaren closing the door behind him, approaching to tell me, regardless of the impossibility of his words, that a wolf prowls the deck, the warm fur of a murderer exploring that narrow space with wild steps and the insane heat of his hunger, stalking?

The *Demeter* a bare forest, which I have inherited upon their death.

Acketz and Joachim shouting, filling me with the formless horror of not knowing what could transform a pair of strong men into broken voices.

"The canvas is alive," they say.

"The fog cleared, Captain, and we could see ... see ...."

"The sails changed color."

"They were black, Captain, torn upon the masts, fluttering in the wind ...."

"Wind that didn't exist ...."

"We knew not how or why they had all been ripped, shredded, yet every piece still hovering together ..."

"... when we touched them, they screamed, all of them."

"And the dark cloth stirred itself, moved of its own accord, throbbing obscenely."

"Then it flew away."

A million bats covering the intact sails, a million membranous wings fluttering in the air, spiraling above us, fading into the storm clouds that—in turn—shouted rain and wind.

The days become confused, days blended with other days by fear, insane goings-on, the silence that slowly covers us without our knowing how.

Did we keep our sanity within that silence, or did we fear we might tear the fragile membrane of normalcy with our voices?

When someone spoke, it was possible to hear his hopeless loneliness, echoing in the immense cavern of the world; so weak, so insignificant that we feared being reduced to that relative whisper.

However, silence also weighs heavy and sometimes, we would risk breaking it in order to breathe.

Vlahutza at the helm started talking to the route, to the wood, to me, about his short stay in Paris.

"I met Martin Dummolard," he said, as if proud of the fact. "I stayed at Justine Lafayette's boardinghouse in Lyon. She was still but a child, then. Fresh meat, as they say, Captain. I slept, unaware there was a pair of murderers in the house. I closed my eyes, never imagining that they both ate human flesh. My father and I left, after paying some coins, ignoring the fate that saved us at that moment. Dummolard was the murderer, cracking skulls to give them to his lover, who sipped their blood as if it were a crime to let it spill, drawing a curved knife to cut away the fleshy parts of the body: the thighs, the arms, occasional breasts that she would eat in her scented room—among the lace and ornaments that have made Paris famous—monstrously swollen, white, like maggots that arise from the flesh. Those who went to arrest her refused to put a hand on her, because touching her might stain one with ignoble liquids. Somehow, the fact that she had been eating only dead bodies for years had turned her into something else. She moved as if her immense flesh were an object that could propel itself as though multitudinous, with the perfect synchrony of insects. There was a trial and evidence and, although it is true that it was more a lynching than a legal execution, it is also true that she shouted until the end of the torment, 'They are meat, meat, meat!' and bit the executioners to taste human blood one last time before burning."

Vlahutza took an old rosary out of his clothes, a coruscating old silver crucifix, which he turned between his fingers, as if it could save him from dreams.

My God, he might have prayed, *deliver me from the memory of my days, from the images you offered to my eyes, from the meaning-laden whispering of Silence round about me. Heavenly Father, offer me the Peace of Ignorance so that the blade that seeks my flesh and blood weighs less before it slays me ....*

He was not unaware that the thin and nervous Dummolard—and his gigantic Justine—wanted him.

They wanted his flesh in the dark, the blood hidden in his veins, the secret liquids of his body.

He wondered what Hunger would come for him in the dark.

"Dost thou desire me, Captain?" he asked in the dark of an endless night.

"Yes," I admitted, as all had already collapsed, and he feared the other crew members, convinced in his heart that someone was preparing cutlery and spices.

He looked at me in such a way that I regretted having confessed it. The world a crack and I an edge that tore at his mind.

"If thou comest for me, I shall kill thee," he said, spitting out the words as if his contempt could cleanse him of my presence.

At that moment, I became Martin to him. My desire is a white and swollen Justine Lafayette between my thighs.

A monster at the heart of the obscene night.

As Mikhail had been a monster, brought down by one of the mob's thousand arms. A shot, a stone, a million shouts surrounding him.

"He killed the boy!" they lied. "He killed the boy!"

Yet, I know, and they as well, that the "boy" was nothing more than a cover for their persecution, a mask affixed to a young man, justifying a rage that needed no more reason than their unbridled fury. Intoxicated by the power of being a mob, by how unbeatable they were before the threat of a single man.

The "boy" had accepted Mikhail's caresses and his *mujik* father preferred to kill his son rather than to accept that his nakedness was not a sin, that caresses offered in the dark, in the glow of the senses, did not indelibly stain *him*.

I might have screamed, might have offered myself, as well, as a sacrifice. But I simply skirted the shores of that surging sea that heaved with the impulse of its communal rage.

Mikhail sank into those human waters and when he fell, he screamed.

Just once.

Vlahutza's scream.

The hoes were raised above his skin, the flesh opening as they fell. Waves: sharp edges rising. Foam: blood spattering the faces, baptizing the crowd with the ignoble ichor of murder.

A baptism that the mob imbibed, satisfied.

He was buried at a crossroads, so that his spirit could not find its way back to the village.

They sank rose thorns in his eyes, condemning him to darkness, even in death.

They filled his mouth with garlic, thinking that—thereby—he could not contaminate anyone with his breath; and what can be kissed while worms gnaw, tireless?

A priest gave the orders; he brandished the long blade that separated head from mutilated body.

He turned it face down; spat a curse into that gaping neck.

Then they nailed the body to the ground with a wooden stake.

The body was a beast for them, the flesh a monster that yielded to an incomprehensible instinct.

What did they really imagine they had stopped with all those rites?

Unimagined pleasure become a whispering silhouette that sought them out, pressing against their windows, touching instincts that had lain dormant for years, convincing their flesh to yield to ... what?

They did not wish to know. They planted heather over his grave, condemning Mikhail to rot in its dreadful roots.

I knew that Vlahutza, had he been a mob one thousand strong, without the route weighing on his soul, would have come at me, with weapons and fury, ready for the rose thorns, the wooden stake, the crossroads where he would leave what remained of me.

"I am not a monster," I told the *Demeter*, gripping the helm in the midst of the fog. "I am not a monster."

But they are.

Petrofsky climbed the *Demeter* from the dark waters, a whisper full of the sea, scratching at the wood and metal of the hull, crawling like a marine insect, clinging to cracks and rust.

First, I saw his hands, searching. I never thought of a shipwrecked man, someone boarding my ship without permission. Such confusion was impossible at the sight of those split fingers— flesh cleaved to the bone, revealing a fleeting white glow—that hurt the ship in their desperation to cling to it.

Petrofsky was the image that all of us who live upon the sea cherish so as not to be seduced by its liquid beauty, by the yawning abyss over which we sail, which offers its depths as a deadly gift, that green formlessness always calling us.

Bloated face, gray and monstrously swollen hands, black lips open to the incessant violation of the waters, in a scream that no one hears, but that still exists in that rictus.

After climbing on deck, he stood there, motionless, mayhap to allow me to drink deep of all the horror offered in the chalice of his body.

I did not scream.

Later, today, I wonder why I didn't scream.

Was that dead man in front of me better than the silence that was wearing me down?

Or is it true what they say, that the worst of horror is that there is no horror? After the signs of the storm, the successive disappearances, the rats and the dreams ... what was a dead man on deck but just a dead man?

Mayhap Justine Lafayette one day reached for her full plate, only to behold that what she ate was no longer a sin, flesh torn from the sanity of the world, but simply something overcooked.

Did she miss the screams of the victims, the fresh blood running down her lips?

Was that why she forced Martin Dummolard to seduce those whom they wanted to eat? Did she make him take them to her boarding house, where she watched from the shadows as they slowly stripped, naked body moving over naked body, killing her victim at the last moment of pleasure?

Was playing with them not what brought joy back to their Hunger?

What details did they exchange while chewing their trophies?

Something to cling to, a symbol that said that the meat was something more, that the dead man on deck was something more.

It was remembering the dark mark around Petrofsky's neck that made me react, which struck the indifference that had saved me from fear.

Not long ago, I yearned for that now-gray flesh, to kiss those now-black lips, to drink the fluids stored inside that now-dead body.

After him, Abranoff climbs aboard, now shouting his despair as he clings to the sails like a huge spider. Olgaren devours the provisions that no longer nourish him, driven by frenetic hunger to chew on lines and cables, seeking the knot that will satiate him. Muresh comes every night to my door, knocking civilly and begging me, in the voice of the one who asks for a small favor, to serve him some meat: *mine*, so that he might nibble, sipping blood with dainty care. Acketz has begun to gnaw one of his own arms, endlessly.

Mayhap the worst of them all is Joachim, who sits in the middle of the deck and groans, as if death itself pains him.

Pale specters within the storm.

I look at them and feel no fear of them. The fact that they are dead and seek my blood is not enough.

How can I fear them when they come together in the dark, pressing against one other, as if they could— so joined—take shelter from the cold, from the night in which they live? Children wounded by the rain.

I watch them shamble through the ship, taking the objects they treasured once, but finding no meaning in them now. Death a blade that cuts reality in such a way that, from the Other Side, our world is nothing more than a collection of senseless things.

Was I one of these? Mere signs of past events, of memories already devoid of meaning?

Never more.

Is that why they drop them, let them break? They know that death is the domain of the lost.

Not only did they lose their lives, their breath, but the whole world, the sun, all that they were.

They move throughout the *Demeter,* looking for the limits of their confinement. But it is not this old schooner that imprisons them. Their prison is not the one that sails through the fog.

They are prisoners of their flesh, locked within their simple appetite for blood, within that basic need.

They are Thirst.

They have defeated death, risen from the grave, and now walk of their own accord. Sometimes, their bodies dissolve into myriad sickly points of light, or their feet become a thousand white rats that, in turn, are transformed into fog and then again are mere feet that cannot take them anywhere. They clamber up the mast like insects and then climb down head first, as if they had no weight and their nails and open fingers were sufficient to support them, yet none of those portents signify. Dark Magic means nothing, because they are Thirst.

They never speak to one another. None has tried to convince me that the Other Side is better, that the black waters of death are pleasant.

How, full of hunger, could they speak of the king-doms of Darkness?

Mayhap they know it not. Not having been invited to the black castle of dissolution, mayhap their supernatural body is the only universe they know.

Mayhap Soul and Flesh have amalgamated into Need.

The priest of Dzerzhinsk always offered us a sermon of hellfire and brimstone: It is necessary to kill the needs of the Flesh to preserve the Soul.

Perdition, he said, *is torturing the Soul through the voice of the Flesh.*

And if they are One?

What if the eternal Soul that they promise us in the churches can be eternal while also being Flesh?

Is Thirst not a small price for such a Gift?

But how to convince those who suffer that Thirst?

My crew left the sea, in the dark, and came search-ing for me.

I saw them approach, living fog, broken flesh, yet full of need. I had to shout, take refuge in madness when I thought of their hands tearing my body open, that vile touch caressing me.

Was it better to jump into the waters, lose myself in the sea along with Vlahutza? Who could know?

But I stayed at the helm, watching as they approached with their insect movements, their mouths filled with thick drool that dripped in slow drabs, anticipating the taste of my flesh.

The only thing I could do, the last thing, was to beg their forgiveness for having embarked on such a cursed journey.

Who has not heard of ships sailing with no one on board? Of steaming meals on tables, cards dealt as though naught had interrupted the game?

What is more terrible: knowing about the disappearance or having almost experienced it?

The sea sometimes needs a sacrifice: the mystery of what happened at the last moment.

Old ships withstand unexpected storms and sturdy boats have been shipwrecked under the sun upon a calm sea.

Is that not the wherefore of our little superstitions: the saliva we spit on the wheel and at the dock, begging them to meet again; the skein Olgaren used to bind the winds; the rosary Vlahutza clutched, commemorating the mysteries; the *mujik* prayers that I have not forgotten; not killing albatrosses; not spilling impure blood overboard; making figures with salt?

I should have taken port when the albino rats appeared, forced Melih to stay on board and confirm there was no danger in the *Demeter*. We should have fled from the endless disappearances.

This is the payment for my indecision: my men rising from their watery grave, coming for me.

The Dark Miracle.

The Secret.

They came out to plunge me into the mystery, so that only the logbook and nothingness might speak of us.

"Yes," I told them, offering myself to them. Is that not what I always desired: to give in to their need, to please their senses, to give peace to their bodies? "Yes."

I had in my hands the rosary that the Mate had dropped at the last moment, as if God were not necessary when surrendering oneself to the oblivion of the sea. They looked upon it as if it were a weapon: the last barrier that stopped them.

This? A dead man on a cross?

The symbol of Soul and Flesh separated. The sign of fear wielded by the priest of Dzerzhinsk, the man who planted a stake in Mikhail's body.

I dropped the beads, let them smash against the ground at my feet.

I would not stop them.

I felt it just that they come for me. An eye for an eye.

My death for theirs.

Blood for blood.

Silver voices, thrumming with a thousand unknown tones, filling each word with the shadow of sounds beyond the human ear.

blood

There was no need for them to say more.

I thought of those pathetic children who have had enough of begging in the ports, so they hide aboard ships, believing that to travel in a hold full of rank cargo is a better destiny.

In exchange for some hypothetical apprenticeship, they cannot offer a strength they do not possess, so they typically give sailors the only thing they can, what they have sold since they discovered they can satisfy a specific hunger.

White and wiry flesh, the caresses of a mouth that has learned that there is nothing more ignominious than hunger.

Cabin boys.

How many times did I fantasize about taking one of them and covering his skin with my lips, making a deal that would give me free use of his flesh?

I never did so because such poor creatures cannot consent. They have no will. They lend themselves to pleasure without pleasure, focused on nonsense while one searches in vain within them for something other than sphincters that tighten mechanically.

One immediately understands that they are not present in that moment, that they have left their body at the mercy of another's need, but that they are safe—or perhaps merely indifferent—elsewhere.

In Bulgaria, they speak of the *obour*, which leaves the grave transformed into a being without bones, of spongy, immaterial flesh, which—sometimes—does not produce shadows because its essence is absent.

When these children lent themselves to the incessant blow of the tides of sex, it little mattered whether they were alive or had become those insomniac specters, scouring the forests in search of what they have lost.

My crew were not *obours*.

I was.

Flesh without will at its disposal.

When we have lost everything, is that not the last thing we possess? Skin and memory.

It mattered not.

They came to me dragging their naked need, stripped of all human traits, dogs looking for fallen scraps.

I knew, then, the terrible price of Flesh and Soul made One.

Eternal Flesh would be a Paradise for a human being.

Yet, what if to reach that place, one must cease being human?

They came to me transformed into monsters. Into Justines. She was human, but not her appetites.

Thirst, I told myself. *They are Thirst.*

To *that* they have been reduced. That is their essence, empty of everything.

Once the hunger was satisfied, with the warm food inside them ... what would they do? Start exploring their new skills, congratulate themselves for having escaped death, stroke their gray flesh?

They could speak of Immortality, of the enormous cycles of time they will witness, of the glacial turning of constellations, of the immobile earth moving through the millennia. Of the Eternal and the beauty of the world beyond the sunlight.

Mayhap they would discover secret senses, new pleasures, the satisfaction of being— incessantly.

Until the Thirst returned.

In the ports of Africa, teeming with the absurdly vital heat of greenhouses, where everything can grow and anything born under the sun seems possible, they sell Ghanaian monsters: deformed creatures with huge teeth so large that, if they should ever clamp their jaws shut, those fangs would pass through their palates to their brains.

They are nothing more than large cane rats fed from birth with liquids, their mouths tied so they can never gnaw and thus file down the ceaseless growth of their teeth.

Ghanaian monsters should die when abandoned to their own fate, but some, the valuable ones, the ones they offer in braided cages, use their disproportionate fangs to rip open other rats and drink their blood, shivering with hunger.

They do not mate.

From the moment their teeth touch another skin to tear it open, there is no other pleasure than to rip, shred the flesh to feed.

That is their true deformity.

Their fangs can break easily, but even without them, they are unable to return to what they never were. They would die in a barn full of grain.

Their paradise: a sea of blood that feeds them endlessly.

My crew, the wraiths that come after my blood with their supernatural form, have been reduced to that: They are Ghanaian monsters with the terrible curse of thought.

"We are sybarites," they might say to one another, afterwards. "Ours is the eternal, immortal pleasure."

But they are nothing more than tortured rats.

And I was their food.

They had to eat of me, break the fragile barrier of my skin and dive into my blood, bathe their hungry faces. Finish in that instant all I ever was.

That would have redeemed me.

But they did not kill me.

*He—**That Thing**!*—prevented it.

The Cruelty That Warps. The Maker of Monsters.

"He is mine," he said, with limitless arrogance.

Then I saw it ... *him* ... in the dark. God forgive me, but Vlahutza was right to jump overboard. It is better to die like a man. To die like a sailor in blue water, no man can object.

My men turned away, abjectly, like dogs at the voice of a murderous Master.

The tall and thin man.

He didn't even bother to approach; far from the helm, looking out at the sea, he growled his order without taking his eyes off the night that made him a vague shadow.

I could feel the power emanating from him, the force contained in each of his movements.

Once, I went to see the Trans-Siberian, the train that—in the long run—is going to kill off the schooners and the captains like me, with its safe rail route crossing a seemingly infinite Russia, bringing passengers and cargo to important ports by land instead of over the formless sea.

Its solid steel, thrumming that thin black skin, all the cars contaminated by the vibrating fire of its locomotive.

I imagined what it would be like to not get out of its way, to stand on the tracks, watching it approach.

That man, that *thing*, had the same strength and also the cruelty of men, as if the Trans-Siberian could jump its tracks at will to snatch up all who thought themselves safe from its fury.

"I am not yours!" I shouted. "I belong to no one!"

And he laughed, softly, without taking his eyes from the black horizon.

"You belong to Mikhail," he said, "and to your small need for pleasure, Captain. You belong to the sin you committed against that man. To the fact that you seduced when he could not rightly choose. You went to him, in the dark, erect, when he could not say *no* to your touch. You went and he accepted, true. And continued beyond your flesh and in the end, he was crushed. You forced him to eat a forbidden fruit and the reward was a stake that forever violates a dead body, with no ceasing, no peace. Nay, you are not mine. You do not *deserve* to be. Captain, you are your own and you serve a very small master."

"How ...?"

"How do I know it all? You told me yourself, in your dreams. You gave me the secrets of your reckoning, of this ship's course, in exchange for a little pleasure. You made a pact with me. The destination of the boat in exchange for the fulfillment of your middling needs. Don't look at me with disgust, little man. You are like me."

He said no more, but continued savoring his voyage, looking out upon a world turned into night, without land, or any human light, to gainsay his dominion.

I should hit him, face him somehow. Channel my fury into weapons, let the steel live its weak tiger dream, let gunpowder explode in my hands as I seek to erase his sneering face.

Vlahutza struck that immaterial flesh in vain.

And *he* knew that I was unable to hurt him. What weapon had I at my disposal?

The crew returned to the water when a gray line appeared on the horizon: the dawn.

The man left his lookout and walked toward the hold, serenely, as if heading to a luxurious cabin.

Why there?

Who would deny him any of the empty cabins, my own bare bed? Yet, he went by his own will down into that rancid hole.

To the boxes we kept there.

I guessed that he rested inside them, that he could only sleep within that oozing earth, among those blind worms brought from his realm, guarded by albino rats.

He went there, sliding, indifferent to the waves and the constant movement of the Demeter. Not as a man of land, not as a man of sea. Something else, different. From kingdoms outside the human experience.

Smiling.

I had worked on enough passenger ships to know that gesture.

I had seen it on the faces of travelers who knew that exotic pleasures awaited them on the other side of the water, unknown but ready to be relished. Only the voyage separated them from new delicacies, from sweet experiences upon their arrival, and therefore the crossing was a pleasure: a long and placid savoring of assured treats.

And what other pleasure could *that thing* desire but other flesh, people disappearing one after another, plunged into darkness?

That *thing* was moving to a new home.

I remembered the Tziganes bringing the boxes, helping that creature onto my ship.

"*Denn die Todten reiten schnell!*"

For the dead travel fast.

To England.

Surely to London, city of four million souls. How much blood there? How many people willing to become like him?

I imagined a world where we are cattle and the banners of the monsters wave over devastated lands, while a million bats in the heavens make the night eternal.

Where ignorant captains take vile seeds on their ships to new shores, in exchange for an ambiguous pleasure.

I screamed, kept screaming, still scream.

When I could calm down, when I forced myself to *be* again, I found again the fog and the insane impulse of the storm, with a myriad of sickly pale moths with incandescent eyes watching me. At night. With my men around me, pathetic in their excessive hunger.

"I did not kill Mikhail," I told them. "Nor did I kill you."

"And you will not kill all of London," said the man, enjoying the voyage, laughing at me.

Hate always feeds on despair. And mine was infinite.

I had to hurt that *thing*. It was my duty to somehow sink into him the selfsame pain he had stabbed into my men, to return unto him the Hunger that had led them to mutilate themselves with their own teeth, which had made them beggars for my meager flesh.

"Blood," they said, like children under the inclement light of a scorching sun.

"Look for other ships," I whispered, damning myself with every word.

I should shut up, let them die again of Hunger.

Was it for them, who obviously suffered, or for me, who could not bear to see them begging, wounded, gnawing at their own hands, that I condemned other crews to darkness?

"We cannot. Water hurts," Olgaren said, finding words difficult, as if he had lost something essential of himself when he died, the flesh in which he found himself imprisoned but a fraction of what it once was—such is not a good grave. Better beneath the *Demeter*.

The sea is a consecrated place for us sailors.

Blessed space where our bones are laid to rest.

But it is something more. Made a sepulcher by the ships that cast their dead into the sea, by the ceremonies carried out on deck.

When they sail away, when the ship is gone, the sea is sea.

The ephemeral magic of the funeral leaves with the boat.

So, the water hurts.

The world outside the grave a place of pain.

I knew, then, what we were transporting to England.

That *creature* could not leave behind the only thing true for every man. He had escaped the funeral shroud, death itself, but not the dark earth of the grave, condemned to always carry it with him.

The memory of dissolution.

Is peace not better: the incessant caress of the earth, of the oozing moisture that will rot away your flesh, obliterating rank as it does memory, destroying what you were, unique, to make you what we all become, dust? Is Rest not a dear-enough payment in exchange for life?

Exactly what would the earth say to that man?

And what did it signify?

He, It, had sealed the hold, closing it from the inside, burying metal and ropes in the skin of the *Demeter* without any effort.

I thought he had locked himself in, but he left at night without difficulty.

Through a crack, I supposed. Like the cracks running along the boxes we transported.

What could I do against him?

Helpless.

"*Tomorrow*," said the man. "Tomorrow, we shall dock."

Fate measured in hours, life like grains of sand that drop to nothingness, revenge lost in blood and flesh beneath the hunger of the victims.

I was going to die with my sin.

"I did not kill you, Mikhail," I said, because all my faith, all my prayers had been reduced that one shaking affirmation.

"I didn't kill him," I repeated a thousand times. After so much silence, so many years of not admitting it to myself, of burying that simple statement in other skins, in other events, on trips along the road of ice and salt, I needed it to bleed from me now.

"I did not …."

"Not …."

I said it so many times, in so many ways, with such force that I ended up listening to myself.

Ended up knowing.

I did *not* kill Mikhail.

"They fear their appetites," he told me once, but it was not true. It was not men wanting men that killed him.

Many secret Hungers (mayhap of flesh, of pleasures, of arrogance or sins) wielded those weapons.

The need to be hidden, to ferment in the dark. Rabidly desired *because* they were forbidden.

The crime a justification.

For the world, for normalcy, so that no one will free the throbbing demons of the flesh, of thought, of who we are behind the masks.

If I have appetites that I consider monstrous ... aren't they all? Is the sin of others not as great as the one I dare not exercise, like the one I perform in secret?

Does it not deserve a punishment I cannot infringe on myself? Do I not kill with rage that which I want to kill inside me, but cannot, because that pleasure, that aberration, that which I treasure is more than I am, more than my own image?

If the Shadow that lives within us could take shape, it would show a void before the mirror: image itself, reflection in a world of unhealthy glow.

I know that Thirst is not evil in and of itself, nor Hunger a stigma that must be erased by fire and blood.

Not even Sin.

It is what we are willing to do to feed an impulse that makes it dangerous.

Who was more monstrous on that country lane in Dzerzhinsk where Mikhail died: he, shot down, or those who expiated their rage upon his body?

I committed a Sin by forcing him to accept my caresses. But I had the incredible luck of being forgiven by his acceptance.

Sleeping together, seeking mutual pleasure in our bodies, should not have ended in blood.

"I'm not a monster," I told the *Demeter*, gripping the helm in the midst of the fog.

I wasn't like *him*, like *it*.

And to prove it, I had to save my men.

Soul and Flesh in One.

What if the Flesh were destroyed? Wouldn't that set the Soul free?

The sea hurts.

And for that am I alive. That is why, on a ship of the dead, I yet breathe.

I discovered it in despair, during days I sailed surrounded by ghosts, during nights when guilt twisted its claws inside me.

A clarity separates me from the man I was before the horror; a clarity achieved in the endless moments of the trap.

I understood it all. I managed to learn it, after I told myself that I was not a monster, when—for naught in particular—I forgave myself for a murder done with weapons I never held.

How to save them, how to save myself, how to destroy the monster.

I knew it when I saw what the tall man observed with such fascination every night ....

I left the helm to the wind and the storm that—I now understand—steers this ship, to the fog that surrounds us like a shroud. But not completely. There were rips here and there, over the sea. I saw the waters flowing fast, the furious foam we created on cutting the waves, the darkness become a liquid body beneath us.

I saw the route that ended, the time that carried me toward that *tomorrow* where I should die.

I saw something white and indescribable under us.

Something *alive*.

Something with a thousand mouths, that wounded the *mind* upon catching a glimpse.

Something that was only able to exist in an insane universe, one where there were tall men looking, fascinated, into the abyss, staring at one of its inhabitants.

I looked away from that monstrous, formless, obscenely multiple silhouette.

I felt that my soul had been stained by that thing, that who I was had died a little more just by seeing it.

"I believe it feels my presence," said the tall man.

I believe.

The moment of revelation.

The ocean is a world that the *creature* did not know. There were secrets, things still hidden from his supernatural gaze.

Living waves that guarded their territories, threatening him with their very existence.

Therefore was I alive.

Therefore did I know how to beat him.

In dreams, I taught him how to calculate the dead reckoning, the course of the *Demeter*, the secret route through the water drawn by maps and stars.

He listened carefully, spent days learning, without touching any of us, even taking care of us. Pushing the storms away, stowing his own, practicing his knowledge.

He was a man of earth, naturally. He had no Tzigane crews to whom he might entrust his safety. He ignored fundamental facts of navigation.

But I taught him.

First me and then mine, in the dark.

But he was a creature of earth, who said *I believe*, referring to something of the sea.

Someone oblivious to the fact that the end is the most difficult part of a journey.

The tide charts, the reef maps, the sandbanks of the coves.

Therefore did he keep me alive.

In the event there was something he did not yet know.

Too arrogant to consider his ignorance might be so vast.

Therefore did he not give me his Dark Gift. What if I lost something vital, as Olgaren had lost his ease with words?

Therefore has he not deprived me of my mobility, not locked me in the forecastle.

He believes me necessary but not vital.

Under the sun, I pull off my clothes. For the first time, I go naked for my men, freeing my flesh from the mask of clothes, stripping myself of what I was, of what I am: A bare body is a body offered to the world, to the weather, to the mercy of fate. Naked we are born, though we strive not to die thus.

Covering ourselves from the world at the moment we leave it.

I do not. I cannot. I leave my flesh free and dive into the sea.

How long traveling the road of ice and salt through how many seas, oceans, climates, and never have I done this—leaping from my boat into the waters.

I immerse myself in the route, leaving behind the universe of wood and canvas, the sanity of ropes and rigging.

Behind me, the voice of the *Demeter*, whispering on her cursed journey, advancing with her sails stained with storm.

I take a breath (sharp, cold air) and let the waters cover me completely.

Diaphanous images before my eyes, ever-changing, as if the sea claims as its own everything that is sheltered inside, even the landscapes beneath its surface. A thousand clear sounds.

This is what the drowned hear.

The vociferous peace of the ocean.

I see my men clinging to the wood of the *Demeter*, like suckerfish protecting themselves from the noon sun in the shadow of the ship.

They see me with their fish eyes, not knowing what I want there.

Children, clinging to one another like puppies, defenseless, with no more security than that of their touching skin.

No longer are they men, nothing more than bare need, mere Appetite.

And are we not all, from time to time?

Can desire not deprive us of everything other than Need?

Was I not like them for many years?

Thus, do I take the knife clenched between my teeth. Because I know I loved them. In that instant.

Mercy is also love; therefore, I open a vein.

The only gift I can give is to kill them.

The only caress worthy of their Hunger.

My blood becomes one with the waters, spreading, a scarlet cloud that surrounds me, that moves toward them.

What is its flavor? Salt upon salt.

As soon as the red cloud touches their flesh, they go mad, their mask of humanity shattered by the craving that, it is said, awakens in hunters the taste of their prey.

Tiger apprentices doing what I always knew they would.

They stop clinging to the *Demeter* and hurl themselves at me, at my flesh, opened for them.

I stop swimming and the schooner moves away.

And the Sea does what it has to do.

Away from their grave, in a kingdom not of their Master, a jealous kingdom.

Is it not said that to kill the *vrolocks*, the *vlkoslak*, the bloodthirsty living dead in Romania, one needs only living water?

In those green depths—caressed by my men, their lips running all over my skin before they begin to feast, shivering with desire for me—I love them before the water performes its task.

Living water, far from the shadow of the schooner, under the submerged light of the sun.

They begin to dissolve.

Arghezi and Muresh, Joachim and Olgaren, Abranoff and Petrofsky, Acketz.

Their skin warmed by my own blood, their members erect sexes from the pleasure of satisfying their Thirst, tongues in my mouth, in my veins, on my cock ... and—

suddenly—the sensations fade. I look at them for a moment, all around me: solid, discernible forms amid those infinite waters, and then ....

The sailors are Lot's wife.

Beings of salt.

I didn't kill Mikhail and knowing it healed my soul. I did kill them and it saved me from guilt.

Flesh and Soul separated.

Dust to dust, into the sea.

Then the line I tied around my waist, linking me to the *Demeter,* pulls taut, dragging me with the speed of the ship, drawing me away from that stain under the sea that is losing shape, devoured by liquid.

I could cut the rope, remain here in the peace of the end, among my dissolving crew.

Free of sin. Blameless.

It is strange how many forms of redemption exist, Mikhail.

But I must see that man for the last time, tell him that Hunger is not a sin, nor is Necessity or Appetite.

What matters, I repeat, is what we are willing to do to satisfy them.

My ephemeral pleasures are not a stain; the fact that he sacrifices others, anyone and everyone else, just to satisfy his Thirst ... most certainly is.

Or mayhap I simply want to spit my triumph in his face.

I have not eaten. I have refused every drop of water. I have bled endlessly among the waters. Even dragged by the ship, I can barely climb aboard the *Demeter*.

Who would think that dying could bring such peace?

Sometimes, I lose whole hours, my sight covering itself with a pleasant darkness, my faltering flesh full of incredible power:

I shall leave him helpless in the midst of the sea, with only my body, and the maps of the coast thoroughly shredded and devoured.

Mayhap he will reach land: It will depend on his luck and on fate.

He will command a dead ship along hungry cliffs.

Voices like dust, surrounding me.

No longer scared, no longer terrible. Not at this moment when everyone has died and I shall, soon.

I have dressed rigorously for those who find my body. Clothes are no longer a mask.

I am what I am.

I write the latest, little space in my shipwreck memory.

A few lines as an addendum to the log.

Still fog, which the sunrise cannot pierce. I know there is sunrise because I am a sailor; why else I know not. I dared not go below, I dared not leave the helm, so here all night I stayed, and in the dimness of the night I saw it, Him! God forgive me, but the mate was right to jump overboard. It was better to die like a man. To die like a sailor in blue water, no man can object. But I am Captain, and I must not leave my ship.

But I shall baffle this fiend or monster, for I shall tie my hands to the wheel when my strength begins to fail, and along with them I shall tie that which He, It, dare not touch: an old rosary.

And then, come good wind or foul, I shall save my soul, and my honor as a Captain.

I am growing weaker, and the night is coming on.

If He can look me in the face again, I may not have time to act.

If we are wrecked, mayhap this bottle may be found, and those who find it may understand. If not ... well, then all men shall know that I have been true to my trust.

God and the Blessed Virgin and the Saints help a poor ignorant soul trying to do his duty ....

Afterword

IN THE WORLD of vampire fiction, there are those who would have you believe that the association of homosexuality and vampirism is a twentieth-century phenomenon, perhaps to be blamed on disaffected 1980s youths with black eyeliner and clove cigarettes. In fact, the first well-known vampire story with obvious gay overtones — Sheridan Le Fanu's lesbian novella "Carmilla" — appeared in the London literary magazine *The Dark Blue* in 1871.

Even when fictional vampires themselves weren't gay, they were frequently used as a metaphor for night-side behavior that included homosexuality. In her essay "A Wilde Desire Took Me: The Homoerotic History of *Dracula*," Talia Schaffer examines the novel's queer subtext, particularly the possibility that Bram Stoker used *Dracula* to explore his own feelings about the ruination of his colleague, friend, and rival Oscar Wilde, who was convicted of gross indecency and imprisoned just two months before Stoker began writing it. Jonathan Harker and Dracula are projections of Stoker and Wilde, Schaffer argues: Harker a married man who initially admires Dracula's intelligence and wit; Dracula "not so much Oscar Wilde as the complex of fears, desires, secrecies, repressions, and punishments that Wilde's name evoked in 1895."

The connection between homosexuality and vampirism, Schaffer tells us, was already well established at that time: "The vampire figure therefore fit easily as metaphor for the love that dare not speak its name. To homophobes, vampirism could function as a way of naming the homosexual as monstrous, dirty, threatening. To homosexuals, vampirism could be an elegy for the enforced interment of their desires."

Sadly, later in life, Bram Stoker became an advocate for censorship. His articles "The Censorship of Fiction" (1908) and "The Censorship of Stage Plays" (1909) target gay themes with coded language like "decadence" and "morbid psychology," referring to "vices so flagitious, so opposed to even the decencies of nature in its crudest and lowest forms, that the poignancy of moral disgust is lost in horror." We cannot know how Stoker, who once called gay poet Walt Whitman "a man who can be if he wishes father, and brother and wife to [my] soul," reached this point, but his disgust and horror at Wilde's plight was certainly an influence. Does such an extreme response indicate gay leanings on Stoker's part? Again, we cannot know, but enough evidence exists to have kept queer scholars discussing the possibility for a century.

In *The Route of Ice and Salt*, José Luis Zárate gives us a queer *Dracula*-related novella taking place aboard the *Demeter*, the ill-fated schooner that brought the Count to England, whose captain was found lashed to the wheel dead with a rosary in his hands. The captain's log traces the crew's disappearance at the hands of some unknown assailant, and the citizens of Whitby treat this captain as a hero, holding a boat parade for his funeral and giving him a Christian burial in the churchyard of the town's famous abbey. In *Dracula*, the log comprises our entire knowledge of this nameless captain. In Zárate's novella, we read the captain's private diary, which begins as an obsessive and fiercely erotic inventory of his homosexual fantasies about his men. As the crew's numbers diminish, he comes to realize that, while he wishes to sexually "consume" the men, something aboard is *literally* consuming them and turning them into vampires. Determined to save their souls, the captain dives overboard and — in a scene containing the gruesome image of the undead crewmen clinging to the underside of the *Demeter* like suckerfish — lures them away from the ship's protection with his own blood, then hauls himself back aboard the schooner to thwart Dracula by dying at the wheel.

The captain is willing to die for his men in part because he believes that his first lover, Mikhail, died for him. Upon learning of the affair, the captain's fellow Russian villagers killed Mikhail in the manner of a vampire, severing his head, filling his mouth with garlic, and burying him at a crossroads with a stake through his body, while the captain escaped. Since this time, the captain has buried his own sexuality, never letting it emerge except in the feverish diary. He is not certain that his death aboard the *Demeter* can redeem him, but he does come to the understanding that homosexuality is *not* vampirism: "Hunger is not a sin, nor is Necessity or Appetite. What matters, I repeat, is what we are willing to do to satisfy them. My ephemeral pleasures are not a stain; the fact that he sacrifices others, anyone and everyone else, just to satisfy his Thirst … most certainly is."

To appreciate the logic of Zárate's novella, it is important to understand that *Dracula* was itself a very sexual book for its day. In his study of the horror genre, *Danse Macabre*, Stephen King characterizes it as "a frankly palpitating melodrama," pointing out that Jonathan Harker nearly experiences oral rape at the hands (and mouths) of the three "weird sisters" who share Dracula's castle. They spare him only at Dracula's command, in obedience to Dracula's claim, "This man belongs to me."

While Dracula never attacks Harker himself, he violates Harker's marriage bed, exchanging blood with Mina while Harker lies in a swoon beside them. Stoker, who was an inveterate self-promoter, sent a signed copy of *Dracula* to British Prime Minister William Gladstone with a note asserting, "The book is necessarily full of horrors and terrors but I trust that these are calculated to 'cleanse the mind by pity & terror.' At any rate there is nothing base in the book." Speculation as to whether Stoker truly believed this or was trying to convince himself along with others is beyond the scope of this afterword. Zárate's captain is far franker about his own desires, but those desires are not out of proportion with those experienced by the characters in *Dracula*; Zárate is simply free to describe them with greater frankness.

In "A Wilde Desire Took Me," Talia Schaffer asserts that "at the heart of [*Dracula*], Stoker gingerly shows that the 'normal' man and the 'depraved' man are one." At the heart of *The Route of Ice and Salt*, then, does not Zárate show that sometimes the "depraved" man must hold himself to a higher standard than the "normal" man simply to stay alive? This idea resonates at least as strongly in today's political climate as it did when Zárate's novella first appeared in 1998. Since that date, same-sex marriage has become legal in the U.S., the U.K. (including Stoker's native Ireland), and Zárate's home country of Mexico, but there are those who would destroy that right and many more. To ensure that doesn't happen, it is vital for marginalized people to see themselves as important citizens of the world, and that includes making them visible in literature and other media, as they are here. Bravo to Innsmouth Free Press for making such a book available, and bravo to you for reading it.

— Poppy Z. Brite,
October 2020, New Orleans, LA

Biographies

JOSÉ LUIS ZÁRATE IS a key figure of the Mexican
fantastic literature of the 1980s. Together with Gerardo
Porcayo, he created the first online Mexican science
fiction magazine, La Langosta se ha Posado, in 1992.
He is a winner of the Premio Internacional de Novela de
Ciencia Ficción y Fantasía MECyF and Premio Kalpa.
Zárate is best-known for a trilogy of short novels centred
around key popular culture figures – Dracula, Superman
and El Santo. He studied Linguistics and Literature and
now teaches a course on fantastic literature in his native
city of Puebla.

David Bowles is a Mexican-American author and translator from south Texas, where he teaches at the University of Texas Río Grande Valley. He has written several books, most notably *They Call Me Güero: A Border Kid's Poems* (Tomás Rivera Mexican American Children's Book Award, Claudia Lewis Award for Excellence in Poetry, Pura Belpré Honor Book, Walter Dean Myers Honor Book). In 2017, Bowles was inducted into the Texas Institute of Letters.

Poppy Z. Brite is the pen name of author Billy Martin, who lives in New Orleans with his husband. His novels include *Lost Souls, Exquisite Corpse,* and *Liquor.* He is currently working on a nonfiction book about religion and spirituality in the work of Stephen King.

Silvia Moreno-Garcia is the author of *Mexican Gothic* and other novels. She runs Innsmouth Free Press and together with Paula R. Stiles won a World Fantasy Award for the anthology *She Walks in Shadows* (a.k.a. *Cthulhu's Daughters*).

9 781927 990292